y Henry Winkler and Lin Oliver

HANK ZIPZER

The World's Greatest Underachiever

The Curtain Went Up, My Pants Fell Down

Grosset & Dunlap

To Lin Oliver: A Writing Partner Sent from
Heaven. And to Stacey always.—H.W.

For my sister, Pamela—with happy
memories of our past and great expectations
for the future.—L.O.

Cover illustration by Jesse Joshua Watson

GROSSET & DUNLAP
Published by the Penguin Group
Penguin Group (USA) Inc., 375 Hudson Street, New York, New York 10014, U.S.A.
Penguin Group (Canada), 90 Eglinton Avenue East, Suite 700, Toronto,
Ontario, Canada M4P 2Y3
(a division of Pearson Penguin Canada Inc.)
Penguin Books Ltd, 80 Strand, London WC2R 0RL, England
Penguin Ireland, 25 St Stephen's Green, Dublin 2, Ireland
(a division of Penguin Books Ltd)
Penguin Group (Australia), 250 Camberwell Road, Camberwell, Victoria 3124, Australia
(a division of Pearson Australia Group Pty Ltd)
Penguin Books India Pvt Ltd, 11 Community Centre, Panchsheel Park,
New Delhi - 110 017, India
Penguin Group (NZ), Cnr Airborne and Rosedale Roads, Albany,
Auckland 1310, New Zealand
(a division of Pearson New Zealand Ltd)
Penguin Books (South Africa) (Pty) Ltd, 24 Sturdee Avenue, Rosebank,
Johannesburg 2196, South Africa

Penguin Books Ltd, Registered Offices:
80 Strand, London WC2R 0RL, England

Text copyright © 2007 by Fair Dinkum and Lin Oliver Productions, Inc.
Illustrations copyright © 2007 by Grosset & Dunlap. All rights reserved.
Published by Grosset & Dunlap, a division of Penguin Young Readers Group,
345 Hudson Street, New York, New York 10014.
GROSSET & DUNLAP is a trademark of Penguin Group (USA) Inc.
Printed in the U.S.A.

Library of Congress Control Number: 2006029450

ISBN 978-0-448-44267-9 (pbk)   10 9 8 7 6 5 4 3 2 1
ISBN 978-0-448-44268-6 (hc)   10 9 8 7 6 5 4 3 2 1

CHAPTER 1

I FELL OUT OF MY CHAIR and rolled onto the linoleum floor. My ears felt like they were going to explode right off my head. They couldn't have heard what they heard. Not the words that just came out of Dr. Berger's mouth. No, those words couldn't be true.

"Hank," Dr. Berger said, looking over the edge of her desk at the floor, where I was still flopping around like a fish with a stomachache. "I wish you'd get back into your chair."

"No way," I answered. "Not until you tell me it's not true."

"I can't tell you that, Hank, because it *is* true. Would you want me to lie to you?"

"Yes," I said, without hesitation. "Yes until infinity."

"No, you wouldn't," she said. "I've made my decision and it's final. I've signed you up for math tutoring with a peer tutor. You start tomorrow."

Peer tutoring! Could anything be more embarrassing?

"Did you say *pear* tutoring?" I asked hopefully, pulling myself to my knees and resting my chin on her desk. "Why would you want me to be tutored by a fruit?"

"You know I said *peer*, not pear," Dr. Berger answered, a smile curling up at the corners of her mouth.

"Okay, I did know that," I said. "I was just hoping it wasn't true."

"Hank, we've had great success with our peer tutoring program, and I believe that being tutored by another student will make math easier for you. So I have assigned you to Heather Payne."

"Heather Payne! I'm double triple hoping that's not true!"

"Well, it is."

That did it! I flopped back down onto the floor again. This was too much information for me to take sitting up. Too much *bad* information.

Heather Payne! Miss Perfect. Miss I'd-Love-To-Do-Homework-For-The-Rest-Of-My-Life. Miss How-Many-Extra-Credit-Problems-Can-

I-Do? Miss I've-Never-Gotten-Anything-Lower-Than-An-A-With-Thirty-Three-Pluses. Oh, no, this wasn't happening.

"Dr. Berger, tell me you didn't say Heather Payne," I said, pulling myself up onto the speckled green plastic chair next to her desk.

"Heather is an excellent math student, Hank, and she has expressed a desire to help tutor a fellow classmate."

"Trust me, I'm not that classmate."

Heather Payne hates me. Well, maybe she doesn't hate me, but she looks at me like I'm some kind of rodent with bugs riding on my back. Once, when I had just gotten back a math test, she glanced at my paper and saw the C-minus written in red on the top. And do you know what she said? "I didn't know they gave grades that low." I had been thrilled out of my mind with that grade. A C-minus was a step up for me. I usually live in D-ville.

Heather Payne is not only a perfect student herself, she's never even hung out with someone who isn't. She was the last person in the cosmos—or whatever is the farthest place from where you're standing right now on planet Earth—that I would want tutoring me in math. Or spelling. Or anything, even sandwich making. I'll bet her idea of making a sandwich is wearing plastic gloves so she doesn't get peanut butter under her fingernails. She wouldn't want to get her fingers sticky because that might reduce the speed at which they can fly across her calculator while she's doing her fourth set of extra-credit math problems. Problems that look like a foreign language to me.

"Hank, I know this is a lot to absorb," Dr. Berger was saying. "Think it over and we'll talk tomorrow to arrange a time you and Heather can work together."

"In other words, 'think it over' means I'm stuck whether I like it or not," I said with a sigh. I can talk that way with Dr. Berger and she doesn't get mad. She's our school psychologist, and she believes kids should be able to express their real feelings as long as they're not being rude.

"I hear your frustration, Hank," Dr. Berger said. "But as I said, we have found that peer tutoring works quite well."

"It won't with me."

"Keep an open mind. It might turn out to be a great experience."

I've found that when adults, even a cool one like Dr. Berger, tell you to keep an open mind, there's absolutely nothing more to say. Anything you say is going to sound like your mind is closed, gone fishing, boarded up. So I gave Dr. Berger my best Hank Zipzer smile, the one that says, "You win for now, but the real Hank will be back with an outstanding Plan B." Then I left her pumpkin orange office, trying to put a bounce in my step. My grandfather Papa Pete says it's important to put a bounce in your step when you're feeling bounceless inside.

Wouldn't you know that the first person I saw when I went out into the hall was Heather Payne, who was delivering the attendance records to the office.

Boy, if seeing her doesn't de-bounce you, I don't know what will.

CHAPTER 2

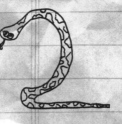

At the first sight of Heather, I flattened myself against the mint green wall, hoping my skin would turn the same green and I'd blend in like one of those chameleon lizards that camouflage themselves when snakes are chasing them.

Please don't see me, Heather Payne. Please don't talk to me, either. Not now. Not later. Not ever.

"Hello, Henry," she said.

Well, I guess that wish didn't work.

I have to tell you, only one other person in the world calls me Henry, and that person is my fifth-grade teacher, Ms. Adolf. No matter how many times I've asked her, begged her, pleaded with her to call me Hank, she refuses. She says she doesn't believe in nicknames. They're too personal. And since Heather Payne loves Ms. Adolf as much as I love Mets baseball and pepperoni pizza, she imitates everything that

Ms. Adolf does. Like calling me Henry.

"It's Hank," I snapped at Heather, trying to slither down the hall. But that girl is not only smart, she's tall. She placed her five-foot-some-thing body in front of my four-foot-something body to block me from taking another step.

"So," Heather went on, "I hear you're going to be my little pet project. I enjoy accomplishing the impossible."

Well, there it was. Heather Payne's first sentence to me, and already I had shrunk from four-feet-something to three-feet-something in a matter of ten words. Her pet project? I felt like a hamster.

"Oh, Dr. Berger did mention we might work together on something, I don't remember what," I answered in my cool guy voice.

"I'm going to be your peer tutor, if you know what I mean."

Peer tutor. The words sounded so horrible, she might as well have said, "I'm going to give you a booster shot," or "You have doggy breath."

"Of course I know what you mean," I snapped. "I happen to be excellent at knowing what people mean. But to tell you the truth,

Heath," I continued in the cool guy voice, "it just doesn't work out with my schedule. I've got football games to watch, a Ping-Pong tournament to attend, an iguana to babysit while my sister has a sleepover with her Girl Scout troop. My schedule these days is chock-full. But hey, thanks, anyway."

I tried to pass her, but she took one giant step and was looming in front of me again.

"But, Henry," she said. "I've already committed to working with you. I even told Dr. Berger that I would step down as the vice president of the Future Physicists of America Club to make sure we have enough time together."

"Oh, wow, Heather, I couldn't let you do that, so let's just forget the whole thing. You go play with your calculator and I'll be on my merry way."

I went left this time, trying to get around her from the other side. At least, I think it was left, since I'm not too good at telling left from right. But she put her arm up like a point guard on a championship basketball team and blocked me again.

"I'm getting community service points for peer tutoring," she said, "and you will look very good on my college résumé, if you know what I mean."

College! She wasn't even eleven years old yet, and she was already thinking about college! Me, I'm just praying I make it to sixth grade.

"I'm not your community service project," I answered. "Try picking up some litter. Or painting the trash cans with happy faces. I hear they give triple points for that . . . if you know what I mean."

This time, I bolted for the stairs at the end of the hall. I was done with this conversation, and I wasn't going to let her block me.

I darted past the bulletin board, past the trophy cases, past the collection of the kindergarten classes' fall leaf drawings that had been on display for the last month. I took the stairs to the second floor two at a time, pulling myself along by the red handrails. I didn't stop until I reached the third door on the left. That's Ms. Adolf's class, better known to those of us who have been at PS 87 for quite a while as the Torture Chamber.

I pushed open the door, which was decorated with . . . well . . . with nothing. Ms. Adolf doesn't believe in decorations, just like she doesn't believe in nicknames. According to her, they both fall under Adolf's Rule Number One, which is "School is for learning, not for fun. If you want fun, go to a playground."

"Oh, Henry," Ms. Adolf said. She looked at me from the top of her gray glasses. Everything she wears is gray, including her face, which unfortunately she wears every day. "Dawdle, did we?"

"No, Ms. Adolf. I came directly here."

"Unfortunately for you, I have done my own research," Ms. Adolf said, looking at her gray wristwatch. "And I know from personal experience that it takes two point three minutes to travel by foot from Dr. Berger's office to my classroom."

"That's providing you don't meet Heather Payne in the hall," I answered. "She insisted on having a long conversation."

"Hey, Zipperbutt, sounds like you and Heather got something going on," a voice shouted from the back row. "That's a laugh! The geek and the geekette."

It was Nick McKelty's voice. He's the school loudmouth who lives to make my life miserable.

10

"What's that stuck between your two front teeth, McKelty?" I fired back. "Is that already-been-chewed oatmeal or have you been gnawing on your math book again and page six got stuck there?"

Everybody burst out laughing. Everybody, that is, but Ms. Adolf, who doesn't believe laughter belongs in the fifth-grade classroom. That's Adolf's Rule Number Two.

"That will be quite enough, Mr. Comedian," Ms. Adolf snapped at me. "Have you forgotten my Rule Number Seven?"

"Not at all," I answered, full of confidence. "Always write your name and the date legibly in the upper right-hand corner of your paper."

"Typical, Henry," she frowned. "That is Rule Number Six."

"You know me, Ms. Adolf. I'm not so great at getting things in the exact right order, but at least I knew the rule."

"Rule Number Seven is that we don't make fun of fellow classmates."

"But McKelty started it. He called me Zipperbutt."

"Henry, if you spent more time on your studies and less time defending yourself . . ."

Before she could finish her sentence, the door to the room swung open and Heather Payne rushed in. It was just like her to rush in after delivering the attendance to the office. Every other normal fifth-grader would take a water break, a bathroom break, and an apple or granola bar break, if they could fit it in. Good old Heather was in a hurry to get back to class, so she wouldn't miss a single solitary minute of her time with Ms. Adolf.

"My, my, my, Heather," Ms. Adolf said. "You were gone longer than usual."

"I'm so sorry, Ms. Adolf," Heather said. "But I ran into Hank, and we had to discuss the arrangements for his peer tutoring."

I thought my ears were going to explode off my head again, right then and there.

Peer tutoring! She said it! In front of the whole class! As if me needing peer tutoring isn't the most embarrassing thing you could say other than, "Oh, Hank, you've just wet your pants."

I think all the color drained out of my face. Well, something drained out of my face, because I felt like I was going to fall over onto the floor. Out of the corner of my eye, I glanced at Katie Sperling, only the second most beautiful girl in our class next to Kim Paulson. She put her hand over her mouth so I couldn't see her giggling. But I could tell by the way her shoulders were shaking that there was a giggle under there. I noticed Kim Paulson's shoulders were shaking, too.

"Heather," I whispered. "Pleeease. Could we talk about this somewhere else or at another time? Like, say a deserted cave in Central Park at midnight?"

"There's no shame in needing help, Henry," Ms. Adolf said. Was her voice especially loud or were my ears just on fire? It sounded to me like she was speaking over the school public address system.

"Shhhh," I whispered to her. But there was no stopping her. She was on a roll.

"Pupils," she said. "Henry is going to be tutored in mathematics. Heather Payne, one of your classmates, will be his tutor. This is how we help one another. One extraordinary student reaching out to help another less fortunate student."

I mean, why doesn't she just hold a big sign over my head that says HANK ZIPZER IS A LOSER!

I had no idea what to do, so the old Hank

Zipzer attitude kicked in. I took a deep bow, as if I had just won the biggest soccer trophy in the history of the sport. McKelty made a farting sound with his hand under his armpit.

"Hank Zipzer has gas in his brain," he shouted.

Everyone burst out laughing. Kim Paulson and Katie Sperling's shoulders shook again. Even more this time.

Holy enchilada! Could this get any worse?

CHAPTER 3

TEN WAYS IT COULD GET WORSE

1. My pants could fall down around my ankles.
2. When they did, everyone would see that I have a rash on my inner thighs from the new laundry detergent my mom tried out.
3. I could start foaming at the mouth for no apparent reason.
4. The foam from my mouth could dribble down my shirt, past the rash on my thighs, and land in a puddle on the floor.
5. I could slip on the saliva puddle on the floor and fall down, knocking myself unconscious in front of everyone.
6. While I was unconscious, my tongue could fall out of my mouth, showing everyone the mushy cream-cheese-and-jelly-on-toast breakfast that had molded itself, McKelty-

style, into every little crevice on my otherwise pink tongue.

7. They could call the paramedics, who would come and refuse to give me mouth-to-mouth resuscitation when they saw the cream cheese and jelly on toast.

8. I would die right there in front of everyone in my class.

9. Which is what I wanted to do, anyway, when Ms. Adolf made her announcement, so the answer is . . .

10. No, it couldn't have gotten any worse.

CHAPTER 4

I COULDN'T WAIT FOR RECESS. When the bell finally rang, I bolted from my chair like a baby zebra heading for the watering hole for a refreshing dip. After Ms. Adolf made her public announcement about my learning issues, I needed a refreshing something, that was for sure.

"Tough morning, huh, dude?" my best friend Frankie Townsend said as we rushed down the stairs toward the school yard. "Adolfosaurus must have gotten up on the wrong side of the bed. And stepped on a pushpin when she did."

"Yeah, how about the way she just blurted out that I have learning problems?" I said. "Next, she'll be telling everyone about my rash." Frankie shot me a look. "Not that I have one," I added quickly. Sometimes you can gross out even your best friend.

"Hey, guys, wait up!" It was Ashley Wong, our other best friend. "What's the big rush?"

"Zip needs to get out to the yard and

blow off some steam," Frankie said. "He's still stinging from the Adolfosaurus attack."

"I don't know why you always get so embarrassed, Hank," Ashley said, falling in step with us. "So you've got learning challenges. But you're extremely resourceful."

"Definition, please, Ashweena. Remember me? Hank Zipzer? Mr. Limited Vocabulary."

"Resourceful. It means you come up with creative solutions to problems other people can't figure out."

"I do? Can you give me an example?"

We had reached the bottom of the stairs where the big glass double doors led to the yard. Everyone was squishing their way through, trying to be first to get outside. I smelled something yucky, like old banana peels and sour milk. Only one person I know smells that bad—Nick McKelty.

"Out of my way, dummy," he said, shoving his way around me. "You're as slow on your feet as you are in math."

As McKelty pushed his hulking frame out the door, he tripped over his own size sixty-two shoes and went down on his rump.

"Don't worry, man," Frankie said. "We

won't tell anyone that you can't walk and talk at the same time, will we, Zip?"

"Especially not Katie Sperling and Kim Paulson," I said, really loud as Katie and Kim passed right by us.

Katie and Kim laughed as they stepped around McKelty. That did give me a little satisfaction. Okay, a lot of satisfaction.

"So, you were about to tell me how I have a lot of natural resources?" I said to Ashley as we walked over to the handball courts.

"Right idea, wrong words," Ashley said. "Natural resources are things like coal and natural gas."

"I have that after I eat beans," I answered, and we both laughed. It's great to have friends who think you're funny.

But before Ashley could go on, a fourth-grader named Zoe Howe grabbed her hand and dragged her over to get in line for handball. So I followed Frankie, who was heading over to the equipment room to check out a ball.

"I can't believe you need to hear compliments, dude," he said, taking a soccer ball from the bin. "Like you don't know your good points."

"I'll tell you what I know," I answered him in

all honesty. "I know that I'm the guy who always seems to screw up—in every subject except for lunch."

I could tell Frankie didn't understand what I was saying. He's so good at everything—school, sports, magic, electronics, even talking to girls— that people say positive things to him all the time. When you have learning issues like me, it can be a long time between positive comments from the outside world. Very loooooong. Dr. Berger once explained that because of the way I feel about myself, sometimes I don't even believe positive remarks when people say them right to me.

"We're losing valuable tutoring time, if you know what I mean," I heard a bossy voice say.

I whipped around and there was Her Tallness, Heather Payne. She was holding a stack of books so big, it looked like she had used up her whole year's limit on her library card.

"It's recess, Heather," I said. "In case you don't know what *that* means, it's a time when kids have fun."

"Ms. Adolf says that fun won't make you a high achiever," Heather answered. I wondered how it was possible for a person so young to act so old.

Frankie dropped the soccer ball on the ground.

"Care to dribble, Zip?" he asked.

"He can't even think about dribbling," Heather answered. "Recess is the perfect time for us to work together. Should we start on decimals, Henry? No, I've got a great idea! Long division!"

Her face lit up like fireworks on the Fourth of July. Wow, I didn't know long division could be such a rush.

"I've got a better idea, Heather," I said. "You go solve the division problems. I'll dribble the soccer ball. And we'll meet up later and compare notes."

"Or not," Frankie chimed in.

"An even better idea," I agreed. "Not."

"Principal Love alert," Frankie whispered to me. "Incoming at ten o'clock."

There he was walking right up to us—our principal, the one and only Leland Love, who has this weird knack of showing up at principal-type moments, like when you're in the hall without a hall pass or about to refuse to be peer tutored.

"What's this little gathering about?"

he asked, giving Heather that special smile principals reserve for the straight-A students.

"I was just trying to get my tutee to come with me to the multipurpose room so we can start our peer tutoring. We're starting with long division."

"Outstanding idea," Principal Love said in his tall-man (even though he's a short man) voice. "There's nothing like making long division your friend."

"I'm really looking forward to doing just that, Principal Love," I stammered, "but my math-problem friend-making time during the day is usually from five after three to seven after three."

"That's only two minutes," Heather pointed out. Leave it to her to get all mathy about it.

"I find that I learn best in short bursts."

Even I had to pat myself on the back. That was an excellent comeback. A *resourceful* answer, if I do say so myself.

Principal Love didn't appreciate my resourcefulness. I could tell because the mole on his cheek, the one that's shaped like the Statue of Liberty without the torch, started to twitch. She does that when he's upset. Once when he stepped on a soggy sandwich and got super-moist tuna salad all over his brown shoes, he was so frustrated the Statue of Liberty actually danced the Electric Slide.

"Look at it this way, young man," Principal Love began. "Heather is volunteering to give up her recess to help you. And helping one another is vital in a society created on the basis of helpfulness. That is to say, helpfulness is essential in accomplishing what it is you wanted to be helpful with in the first place."

Huh?

Leland Love has a way of speaking English so it sounds like a language you've never heard before. And this was a classic Principal Love-a-thon. We were all speechless, even Heather.

"Therefore," Principal Love continued, very happy with the sound of his own voice, "I suggest you find your way to the multipurpose room, so Heather can get on with the business of being helpful."

Even though I didn't understand a lot of what he said, there was one thing I did understand loud and clear.

From now on, recess was going to totally suck.

CHAPTER 5

I FOLLOWED HEATHER to the multipurpose room, walking as far behind her as I could. My feet wanted to go fast, but I kept telling them to slow down.

"Do you always walk this slowly?" she asked me.

"My feet are refusing to cooperate," I answered. "I guess they don't like long division any more than my brain does."

Looking around the empty multipurpose room, the only word that came to mind to describe it was "dungeon." It was dark and cold and empty in there, with chairs stacked around the sides of the walls. It looked like a hold of an Egyptian ship I saw once in a movie, where the men were chained to their oars and had to row for days with no food.

I've had some good times in that multipurpose room. The International Day food festival we had there last year was a lot of fun, especially when Ms. Adolf ate my spicy enchiladas and got the gas attack of the century. The awards ceremony for the School Olympiad, when I got my first and only gold medal for pitching on the winning softball team, took place right in that very room. And kindergarten graduation was a blast, when we all wore caps and gowns made out of paper grocery bags. That was the day Frankie, Ashley, and I swore to always be best friends.

But as I stood there watching Heather set up two plastic chairs on either side of a long wooden table, those fun memories seemed to fade right out of my mind. The only thought in my head was, *Help, somebody get me out of this dungeon right now.*

Heather sat down on one of the chairs and motioned for me to sit down across the table from her.

"Where should we start?" she said, pulling out our math workbooks from the huge stack of books she had carried in there. "We can either begin with Chapter Five and go back to Chapter One, or we can start at Chapter One and move right through to Chapter Five."

"Are those my only choices?" I asked.

"Come on, Henry, this is your tutoring session, too. I want you to have some say in this."

"Then my first choice is that you call me Hank."

"If that will help you learn, then Hank it is. You see how easy this is? We've already made a decision together. Now I'll make one. Let's start with Chapter One."

"Couldn't we just study the cover for a while?" I asked, hoping to stall until the bell rang. "Let's look at all the funny pictures. Like this number five with little yellow legs. Where do you think it's running?"

"Hank, this is off topic, if you know what I mean."

"Maybe it's running a marathon," I went on. "I know. Number five is determined to beat nine. Oh, wait, nine isn't even in the race, because seven ate nine."

Man, I love that joke. I cracked myself up and let out a huge chuckle. Midway through my chuckle, though, I noticed that Heather wasn't even close to chuckling. In fact, she stood up, which took her a long time because she's so tall, and put her hands on her hips.

"Hank, are you going to be serious about

this, or what?"

"I'm definitely going for the *or what.*"

"Okay, you can sit there cracking jokes with your D in math, or you can come with me as I lead you down the path to mathematical excellence."

"I've been down that path and there's man-eating goats on it. I'd much rather go down the path to an excellent lunch."

I know, I know. I was giving poor Heather a really hard time. But it's not because I was enjoying being a jerk. My real goal was to avoid even attempting a math problem, because I didn't want her to see how really, truly rotten I am at math. My brain is just not math-friendly. As a matter of fact, it totally doesn't work in the number area. It's not too hot in the letter area, either, but that's another story.

I'm not exaggerating about how much I stink at math. Take the other day when I went to the drugstore to get a package of tropical fruit Life Savers. While I'm opening it up to search for the mango one, Peggy, who is the owner of the store, handed me change, but I couldn't even tell if the change in my hand was correct. I didn't know how much I was supposed to get back in the first place. Lucky for me, Peggy is very honest, so I knew I was getting back the right amount. But still, it's totally embarrassing not to be able to do what any second-grader can do.

So, I think you can understand why I wasn't exactly excited about showing Heather Payne my math skills. Cracking jokes came much easier. If only making up jokes was a subject in school, I know I'd get an A.

"Hank, you just refuse to take anything seriously," Heather said. "I enjoy taking things seriously. That's because I am a serious person!"

"And an impassioned one, too!" came a man's deep voice from the other side of the multipurpose room. "I like to see the spark of anger in the eyes. Anger is fuel for the soul."

"Huh?" said Heather, almost before she could help herself.

It was the first time I had seen her speechless. I had no idea who this man with the big voice was, but I liked him right away. Anyone who could shut up Heather Payne was my new best friend.

The man walked across the room to our table. Well, I guess you can call it walking. It was more like floating. You hardly saw his legs moving. It was like his shoes had wheels. He was wearing a black cape that flew out behind him, almost like Superman's, except there was no *S* on it. He had shiny black hair and a black goatee. He looked like one of the Three Musketeers. That's a really hard book that my sister Emily is reading right now. I can't read it, but I love to look at the pictures. I like guys with capes and swords and cool hats with feathers sticking out of the top. Those guys look like they can take care of business.

The Musketeer walked over to us, and I noticed he was being followed by Mrs. Crock, who works in our school attendance office. She's really nice. She's so nice that I don't even let myself laugh when she has a big wad of green lettuce stuck in her teeth, which is pretty much all the time. Mrs. Crock likes salads.

"Well, hello there, Hank and Heather," Mrs. Crock said with a smile.

Yippee. No lettuce.

"I'd like you children to meet Devore," Mrs. Crock went on. "Or is it Mr. Devore?"

"Simply Devore," the Musketeer said.

"Children, Simply Devore is going to direct our winter musical."

"No, my dear Mrs. Crock," he said. "It is merely Devore."

"Oh, so sorry," she said. "Merely Devore is going to direct our winter musical. He'll be working with us for three weeks. Aren't we lucky?"

"Mrs. Crock," he said, his deep voice echoing around the multipurpose room like one of those Swiss yodelers on TV. "Repeat after me. Devore. Period. Devore and nothing else. Just one name."

"Oooohhh," she said, looking a little embarrassed. "I get it now. My brother-in-law works with a fellow at the toothbrush plant that has a younger brother who only has one name, which, if my memory serves me correctly, is Sampson."

"Wow," I said. "What part of the toothbrush does he work on? The bristles or the handle?"

Heather shot me an annoyed look, but Merely Devore didn't.

"This boy has a curious mind," he said, waving his cape at me. "Curiosity is the key that unlocks drama. What is your name, young man?"

"Hank Zipzer. With two z's."

"And you're a speller, too! I love a linguist!"

"Well, I really wouldn't go that far. My

30

spelling goes downhill after my name."

"Mr. Devore," Heather said. "I mean Devore. We only have a few minutes left, and Hank and I are working to improve his math skills. He is my tutee, if you know what I mean."

"Could you please not call me that in public?" I whispered, trying not to move my lips.

Devore turned to her, his cape sweeping in a circle behind him.

"How perfect," he said. "You have the instincts of a teacher. Just like Anna in my musical."

"Devore is directing *Anna and the King of Siam* as our winter musical," Mrs. Crock said. "He wrote a special script just for PS 87, based on the book."

"Oh, I read the entire book over the summer," Heather said. "Twice."

"Very impressive," Devore said. "How did you know over the summer that *Anna and the King of Siam* was to be the subject of our winter musical?"

"It was listed in the PS 87 master calendar," Heather said. "Both online and hard copy. I study the calendar carefully, so I'll be prepared for each and every event."

I watched Devore's eyebrows shoot up so high

they almost touched his shiny black hair. He was getting his first blast of Miss Perfect.

"Well, you certainly seem like a competent young lady," he said. "Very much as Anna is, in the play."

"That's why I'm trying out for the part," Heather said. "I think I could play Anna. I'm told my leadership qualities are superior."

"We shall all find that out at the auditions tomorrow," Devore said. "But your confidence inspires me."

I think Heather Payne blushed. No! Does Heather Payne blush? Not possible. It was probably just because it was cold in the room. My mom's cheeks get rosy when she walks in Central Park in the winter.

"And you, Mr. Double Z," he asked, turning to me. "Can I expect to see your smiling face at the auditions?"

"No, I'm not the drama type," I said, which was code for what I really wanted to say, which was, "There's no way I could read a script out loud in front of the other kids."

"Oh, Hank, you have a wonderful personality," Mrs. Crock said. "I think you'd make an adorable King of Siam."

"I don't even know where Siam is," I answered.

"It's in southeast Asia, bordering Myanmar, Laos, Cambodia, and Malaysia," Heather, Miss Encyclopedia, piped up. "Approximately the size of France, with a capital city of Bangkok, today it is known as Thailand."

"I love Thai food," I said.

"You see, young man," Devore said. "You are already connected to the material."

"Wow, I didn't know shrimp toast made me an actor."

"Well then, I expect to see you at the auditions," Devore said.

I shrugged.

"Perhaps you could prepare a scene with Mr. Double 7," he suggested to Heather. "What do you say?" he said, turning back to me. "Am I awakening the inner actor who lives inside you?"

Fortunately, the bell rang before I had to give him an answer. I grabbed my backpack, and my inner actor and I ran off to class.

CHAPTER 6

I RAN ALL THE WAY from the multipurpose room to Ms. Adolf's class. I bolted into the room, jumped into my seat, folded my hands on my desk, and looked straight ahead.

Hank Zipzer, reporting for class.

Then I looked around. I noticed that all the desks were completely empty.

"Henry," Ms. Adolf said. "Once again, you haven't looked at your schedule. You are supposed to be in music class with Mr. Rock."

"I knew that, Ms. Adolf," I said. "I just thought I'd stop by to see how you were doing. Gosh, you look rested. So, I guess I'll be going now. Bye."

I grabbed my backpack, and my inner actor and I ran off to music class.

CHAPTER 7

Mr. Rock's music class meets twice a week right after recess. At least, I think it's twice a week. I'll have to check my schedule and let you know for sure. As soon as I find it, that is.

By the time I got there, everyone was in their seat and Mr. Rock was already talking. The thing that's so cool about Mr. Rock is that he didn't stop class and embarrass me by wanting to know why I was late. He just said, "Take a seat, Hank. Good to see you."

What a relief it always is to be in Mr. Rock's class. First of all, it's great to have a teacher who really and truly *is* glad to see you. Second of all, he puts interesting things all over the wall for you to look at in case your attention wanders, which mine has been known to do. Like the poster of a cherry red vintage Corvette over his desk. And weird instruments, like a fish-skin talking drum from Africa and a yak jawbone that they use as a flute in Mongolia. And third of all, you don't have to sit in rows. He has the chairs arranged in a horseshoe, which he says makes for better communication.

Frankie had saved the seat next to him for me. As I sat down, I noticed that on the other side of me was Heather Payne. I wondered if she was like a human magnet, pulling me toward her like two asteroids on a collision course. No, the solar system wouldn't do that to me. It's my friend.

"So, Hank," Mr. Rock said, "I was just telling the class that today I'm going to show you guys an excerpt from a movie called *The King and I*, which was a Broadway play before it was a movie. The movie and the play are based on a book called *Anna and the King of Siam*."

"Excuse me, Mr. Rock," I interrupted, "but isn't Siam what we call Thailand today?"

Heather shot me a look that said, "Who are you kidding, buddy? I just told you that five seconds ago." I looked the other way. This was no time to make eye contact with her.

"Very impressive, dude," Frankie whispered to me while Mr. Rock was putting the video-tape in the machine. "When did you become a geography whiz?"

"My dad has a subscription to *National Geographic*," I said.

"I thought you just looked at the pictures."

"I've moved on. Now I read the captions under the pictures, too."

"I've selected this excerpt for you to see," Mr. Rock said, turning back to us, "because the winter musical, which will be held in three weeks, is presenting an adaptation of this story."

"I'm going to audition to play Anna," Heather volunteered.

"Good for you," Mr. Rock said. "Our director, Devore, has asked me to encourage all of you to audition. I'm going to work with him as musical director, and we want everyone to participate in this very exciting production."

"Not me," Ashley said. "I can't sing worth beans."

"Putting on a play requires so many different talents, Ashley," Mr. Rock said. "For instance, we need a stage manager to be in charge of the production . . ."

"Did you say in charge?" Frankie asked. "Then you got your man, Mr. Rock."

"We also need people to build and paint the scenery and to design costumes . . ."

"That's me," said Ashley. "I found my job. Did they wear rhinestones in Siam?"

Ashley loves to bejewel all her clothes with rhinestones. In fact, that day she was wearing a blue T-shirt with three purple rhinestone dolphins on the front. Dolphins are her trademark, but she also decorates with turtles, fish, and baby hippos.

"Not only did they wear rhinestones in Siam," Mr. Rock said, "but the royal clothes were often made of cloth spun from real gold."

"Wow," said Ashley. I could see her mind start to swirl with excitement.

"The scene I've chosen to show you is when Anna, who is a governess, arrives from England," Mr. Rock explained.

"Is a governess like a lady governor?" Luke Whitman asked, taking his finger out of his nose just long enough to finish the question.

"No, a governess is like a tutor."

A tutor! Could someone please stop using that word around me?

Before I could stop myself, my eyes locked on Heather's eyes. She gave me a little smile, as if we had some sort of secret connection. This was not okay with me. It's one thing to be tutored by her. But it's quite another for her to think she could get away with making little smiley faces at me.

If Heather Payne thinks I'm going to smiley-face back, then she doesn't know everything she thinks she knows.

"Anna has been brought from England by the King of Siam to teach his nineteen children," Mr. Rock was saying.

"Nineteen kids!" Ryan Shimozato called out. "It's a good thing they didn't live in my apartment!"

"At first, the king and Anna do not get along at all, because he isn't used to a woman being so independent. But eventually they fall in love."

"There's not going to be any kissing in this, is there?" Luke Whitman asked. "Because I can't be in a play where there's kissing."

"You won't have to worry about that, Luke," Kim Paulson said. "The area under your nose is not exactly a Kiss Me zone."

"But mine is," bellowed Nick McKelty like the water buffalo he is.

"You wish," Ashley said.

"Well, I just want everyone to know now. I am playing the king," McKelty hollered out in his usual bully voice.

"Not necessarily, Nick," Mr. Rock said. "That's why we have auditions. To find out who is right for what part."

"Come on, Mr. Rock," McKelty said. "We all know that auditions for the part of the king are a waste of time. I mean, look at me. Do you see anything else here but a king?"

What I saw was a thick blond lug with size sixty-two feet who had taco sauce running down the front of his shirt.

"Let's just watch the tape, shall we?" Mr. Rock said.

I settled back in my chair and watched the video. I was prepared not to be impressed. Once when my grandpa Papa Pete was babysitting for us, he made us watch a DVD of an old Broadway musical and invited our neighbor Mrs. Fink to come over and watch it. They sat singing along really loud to songs that had never ever been on MTV. I love Papa Pete, but I have to say, that night definitely did not make the list of my top three favorite evenings.

But this movie, *The King and I*, was different. I mean, the guy who played the king was cool. He was completely bald and completely buff, like the slickest wrestler you've ever seen. He walked around barefoot in these puffy golden pants, flexing his muscles and looking powerful. And his voice! Wow, that voice! It sounded like Darth Vader would sound if he could sing.

I didn't take my eyes off the screen. I was totally hooked. That guy was me, and I was him. I had those muscles inside my arms. I had that voice inside my throat. True, I didn't have those cool golden pants inside my closet. But that could be arranged.

By the end of music class, I had made my decision.

Watch out, McKelty. I was going to be King of Siam.

CHAPTER 8

WHEN I GET SOMETHING in my head, I really get it in my head. I mean, once it's in there, it's not going anywhere else soon until it's done. Papa Pete calls this tenacity, which means that once I decide to do something, I see it through to the very end. There's no stopping me.

So when I decided that I was going to play the King of Siam, the idea crawled into my brain and took up permanent residence there. From the moment I saw the video, I *was* the King of Siam.

"Turn green," I ordered the stoplight on the corner of Amsterdam and 78th as my sister, Emily, and I walked home after school that day. "The King of Siam commands it."

"Apparently, the light doesn't obey foreign royalty," Emily said.

Oh yeah? Well, at that very moment, the red light turned green, which shows you how much Emily knows about the power of the king.

When we arrived at our apartment, I pushed the front door open and announced to all that could hear, "The king has arrived. Please show the proper respect."

The only person who responded wasn't a person at all. It was Cheerio, our family dachshund, who came running up to greet me, spinning in crazy circles like he always does when he's excited.

"At least the royal puppy shows me some respect," I said, scratching him behind both ears at once.

Emily wasn't having any more of my kingly games.

"Hank, would you please get out of the doorway so I can get into the apartment? Some of us actually have homework to do. But I guess you wouldn't know about that."

I hope that you never have to put up with a smart sister, because they are really difficult to live with.

"The king grants you permission to pass this one time," I said. "But please show the proper respect in the future."

"Hank, breaking news. You're not a king," Emily said in her know-it-all voice. She pushed by me and shook her head all the way down the hall to her bedroom.

"I will find the appropriate punishment for you, peasant woman," I called after her.

As I hung up my green jacket on the coat-rack by the door and dropped my backpack in the hall, I shouted again, just for the fun of it.

"Hear ye, hear ye, loyal subjects, the king is home for his royal snack."

Unfortunately, the only loyal subject who heard me was my dad. He was sitting at the dining room table doing whatever he does on his laptop. I'm still trying to understand exactly what he does for a living. I know it involves computers and long columns of numbers, which as we know, I am allergic to. One number, like ten or even fifteen, is okay with me. But when that number becomes a huge pile of numbers, I get a purplish rash on my knees, which is really tough to scratch through my jeans.

I walked through the living room, stepping carefully over Cheerio, who was still spinning in circles around my feet. When I reached the dining room table, I saw that my dad had set out an after-school snack for me—a granola bar and a glass of milk.

"Ah, the juice of the cow," I said, picking up the milk and gulping it down. "To express his thanks, the king will have a sack of gold delivered to you."

"Enough of your clowning around, Hank," my dad said, looking around the table for his reading glasses, which he finally found on top of his head. "I have a message for you."

"Ah, another one of my loyal subjects wanting my advice?" I asked, a little less kingly this time.

"Heather Payne called," my father said, reading her name from a scrap of paper he had torn off the bottom of one of his crossword puzzles.

"Whoops, wrong kingdom," I said, heading for my room as fast as my royal feet could carry me.

"Stop right there," my dad said. "I am not finished. Her message was that she wants to set up a tutoring time. She said she was your peer tutor in math."

I ask you, how about that Heather Payne? She should change her official name to Heather "I'll-Just-Blab-About-Hank's-Personal-Business-To-Anyone" Payne! What was she thinking? Is there anyone in this whole city she hasn't told yet? Maybe the guy who runs the elevator in the Empire State Building wants to know about my long division skills, or lack of them.

"What's all this about peer tutoring?" my dad asked me.

"Oh, it's an experiment that Dr. Berger thought up," I said, trying to make it sound like everyone in the school was giving it a shot.

"Apparently, it's more than an experiment if Dr. Berger feels you need it."

"Okay, Dad. I'll tell it to you straight. I didn't exactly ace my last math test."

My dad took off his glasses and stood up. I'll be honest with you. I didn't like the standing up part. I didn't feel it was necessary.

"How bad, Hank?"

"Let's just say I took the long way around long division, and it led nowhere," I said.

"You failed?"

Not only was my dad standing up now, he was bending down so his face was directly in front of mine. And let me tell you two things about his face. One is that his face looks a lot like mine, only older. And two is that his face definitely didn't look happy.

"I don't think a D-minus is technically in the

failure category."

"Hank, have you no pride?" he said, starting to pace up and down on the Oriental carpet. "If you just sat at your desk and concentrated instead of playing toe basketball or any of those other silly games you dream up, you wouldn't have to suffer the embarrassment of peer tutoring."

I didn't answer him because I couldn't tell him he was wrong. I mean, yes, I was suffering from embarrassment to have to be peer tutored. And it's even more embarrassing that Heather was telling everyone in the world. Most embarrassing was that I just couldn't figure out why my brain didn't work like everyone else's.

"We have to start cracking down on you, Hank," my dad said. "Failing math is not acceptable."

Oh boy, I didn't like where this was going. I hoped it wasn't going toward the subject of TV.

"I think I'm going to have to start limiting your television watching, young man," he said.

Look at that, that's exactly where it went. I'm a mind reader.

"When is your next math test?"

"Two weeks from Friday," I answered. I knew that because it was a big unit test on long division. Ms. Adolf had mentioned it every day that week.

"Fine," my dad said. "Between now and two weeks from Friday, there will be no TV, except maybe an hour on the weekends."

My heart was going thumpity-thump, and not in a good way.

"Does that include video games?" I asked. "Because technically they're not really TV, they're just digital games played on a TV screen."

I thought I'd wowed him with my excellent and very resourceful point. Apparently, he was wowless.

"Let's see what it's like for you to have two solid weeks of no distractions," he suggested. "I'll pick you up tomorrow right after school. I'll walk you home. And you'll get right to work studying math."

"Gee, that sounds swell, Dad. But tomorrow after school are the auditions for the winter musical. I'm trying out for the part of the king."

"This is a prime example of your priorities,

Hank. A musical is an extracurricular activity, and can in no way get in the way of your math."

"But Dad, it's a school function. Being in a play is part of my education."

"Nonsense," my dad said. "Your future will not depend on you being in a play. But it will depend on how proficient you are in mathematics."

"Dad, I can feel it in my bones. I'm going to get the lead. I'm going to be the king. You can't stop me from trying out. You have to let me try out."

My dad paced up and down on the Oriental rug some more. Cheerio had stopped spinning and had started chewing on my socks. The only sound in the room was the grinding of his cute little teeth as he chomped away at my sock's elastic. My dad was rubbing his chin, something he does when he's thinking hard.

"All right, Hank," he said at last. "If you want to be in this play so badly, I'll make a deal with you. When is the musical?"

"In three weeks."

"And your math test is in two and a half weeks? So it's before the musical."

"Right you are, Dad. You're pretty good in math, I must say."

I gave him a big smile, which he didn't return.

"Okay, Hank. You can try out tomorrow. And if you get the part, you can play the king."

I threw my arms around his neck.

"Dad, you're the greatest," I said, hugging him with all my might. "I knew you'd understand."

He unwrapped my arms from his neck, and held my face in his hands. I thought he was going to give me a kiss. But instead, this is what I got.

"If you get a B-plus or better on your math test, you can continue in the play," he said. "If you get lower, you will have to immediately drop out."

"It's a deal," I said, without even thinking.

I danced around in a little circle, and Cheerio twirled around with me. Then I picked up Cheerio and ran into my room before my dad had a chance to change his mind.

I sat down at my desk. I spun my chair around, and as I was doing a three-sixty turn, it hit me like a wet noodle right across the face.

A B-plus.

The last time I got a B-plus . . . was . . . let me see . . . oh, right, it was in . . . "plays well with others."

And that was in preschool.

How was I ever going to get a B-plus?

CHAPTER 9

TEN THINGS THAT WOULD BE AS DIFFICULT AS ME GETTING A B-PLUS ON MY MATH TEST

1. I could hold a rope between my teeth and pull the family minivan with the whole family in it (including Cheerio) all the way out to Aunt Maxine's on Long Island while singing *Yankee Doodle*.
2. I could hop across the Manhattan Bridge upside down while standing on one hand, right into my favorite Chinese dumpling restaurant, and eat two dozen pork dumplings with my toes.
3. I could use a diving board to spring into outer space, where I would land on Mars and send back photographs of me doing the cha-cha with a bunch of Martian girls.
4. I could root for the Yankees to beat the Mets in the World Series.

Nope, I could never do that. That's just not possible. Not ever.

5. I could keep my sock drawer neat and organized.

   Nope, that's not possible, either.

6. Okay, I could live in an igloo in the North Pole for a whole winter, eating whale blubber sandwiches on Wonder bread, wearing only a bathing suit.

   Actually, that sounds more doable than getting a B-plus on my math test.

7. I can't go on with this list, not because I'm out of ideas, but because my father is yelling through the door that Heather Payne called to say we're meeting tomorrow morning before school to go over . . . yes . . . long division. Oh, Heather, will you ever get a life?

CHAPTER 1

IF YOU THINK THAT SEEING Heather Payne first thing in the morning is going to put you in a good mood, then you're probably the type of person who likes to break their leg and walk around on it without crutches. But there she was, at school bright and early the next morning, waiting for me at the round table in the corner of the library—book open, pencil in hand.

"Ready to work on some long division?" she chirped like a twiggy cricket.

"I can hardly wait," I said, sitting down on a blue plastic chair that she had pulled up real close to her. I pushed it back some. I like to keep some personal space between me and long division.

"Hank, why do you have such a poor attitude about math?" she asked.

"Because I can't do it," I answered.

"Long division, like all forms of mathematics, is just about remembering a logical sequence of steps, if you know what I mean," Heather said.

"Well, in this case, I don't know what you mean, because what's logical to you isn't necessarily logical to me."

I wasn't being a smart aleck. I was just trying to give her the picture of what happens inside my head when I see a math problem on the page. The first thing that happens is that I feel nauseous. Then my brain goes numb, like the way your arm feels when you sleep on it—except my brain doesn't tingle, it just lies there in my head, staring at the problem and having no idea where to begin.

"I'll walk you through the steps," Heather offered. "For the first problem, we'll try a simple one. What is seventy-five divided by five?"

"Forty-five," I said, without a second of hesitation.

"Why did you say that, Hank?"

"Because forty-five is Pedro Martinez's number."

"Who is he and what does he have to do with long division?"

"He's my favorite pitcher for the Mets, and he's got nothing to do with long division, but he happens to be one of the best pitchers in the big leagues."

"Hank, watch me as I solve this problem," Heather said, picking up her pencil. "And please, concentrate."

She started scribbling numbers down on a piece of notebook paper, talking in strange tongues as she wrote. She was throwing words around faster than Pedro Martinez's fastball.

"You take the first divisible digit in the dividend, divide it by the divisor, and place the quotient up here," she said.

Excuse me, Heather. Are you speaking Greek? Or is it Russian?

"Then you just multiply the quotient by the divisor. Subtract the product from the dividend, compare the difference to the divisor, and bring down the next digit. Are you following?"

I started to laugh.

"What's so funny?" Heather asked, looking more confused than angry.

"I don't know why you decided to teach me long division in Russian," I said, "because that's what those words sounded like to me."

"They are common mathematical terms, Hank."

"Maybe to you. But to me, they sound like Russian or Greek or Chinese or maybe one of those strange African languages like Swahili where they make those cool clicking sounds with their tongues. That I can do."

I made a couple of tongue clicks that I thought sounded definitely authentic.

"Hank, please stop fooling around or we're never going to get anywhere."

"Heather, on my honor, I am not fooling around. I am trying to understand what you're saying, but I can't."

"It's not hard, Hank."

"Heather, maybe not for you. It makes me crazy that it's so easy for you, and all it sounds like to me is gobbledygook. I feel so stupid. So totally, hopelessly stupid."

Did I just say that to Heather Payne? I just admitted the thing that makes me feel the worst in the whole world to . . . this very tall, very perfect girl.

Heather got real quiet for a minute. I could tell she was thinking about what I said. I was thinking about it, too, and wondering why I had just spilled the beans about something so personal to someone I hardly knew. Then Heather said an amazing thing. An amazingly *nice* thing.

"You're not stupid, Hank," she said. "Maybe

I'm the stupid one, if I can't figure out a way to teach you this."

We both just sat there in the library, listening to the big clock on the wall tick off the seconds. The only other sound was the librarian, Mrs. Frishman, typing on her computer keyboard at the other end of the room.

"Let's try it again, but without the fancy math words," Heather said at last.

She wrote the problem down again.

"Now, first step. How many times does five go into seven?"

"I have no idea."

She got up and went to the bookshelf and brought back a stack of books. She laid out seven of them on the table, then she gave me five books.

"Now place each of these five books on top of each book on the table."

I did that. Five books were covered, and two were left uncovered. I looked at the table for a while, and then it dawned on me! I could see the division right there in front of me. On the table!

"Five goes into seven one time, with two books left over," I said.

"Absolutely correct, Hank!" Heather screamed,

jumping around like a baby monkey who just got a banana. A very tall baby monkey. Mrs. Frishman looked up and was about to tell us to settle down and use our library voices, but when she saw why Heather was so excited, she didn't say anything. She's really nice.

Seeing the answer to the math problem right there in front of me was like a door opening and letting light into my big, dark brain. My head couldn't visualize the numbers on the page. Or understand the fancy math words. But it could see the books, count the books, and figure out the answer that was right in front of my eyes!

Heather and I went on with the problem, making stacks of books and adding and sub-tracting new books, working the problem all the way through to the end, until I figured out that five goes into seventy-five fifteen times.

That's right. I, Hank Zipzer, solved a long division problem. It took a ton of books—one whole library shelf was on the table—and fifteen minutes, but who cares? I not only got the right answer, but for the first time, I actually under-stood what division was all about.

When I was finished, I was so excited, I jumped up and down, too, and nearly hugged

Heather. *But*, and this is a big *but*, I caught myself just in time. If I thought admitting to her that I was stupid was bad, hugging her was totally off the chart and out of the question.

"That was so satisfying, Hank," Heather said as we put the books back on the shelf. "I feel like I actually taught you this process, if you know what I mean."

Yes, Heather Payne! I do know what you mean! I really do!

"Heather," I said, flashing her my super-duper smile that shows my upper and lower teeth, "there might actually be a B-plus in my future."

"What's so important about getting a B-plus?"

"It's the only way my dad is going to let me be in the school play. I'm going to audition for the king."

"You'll be great at that, Hank," she said. "You're so funny and you're a natural leader. I'm going to try out for Anna, but I bet I won't get the part. Probably all the other girls are going to try out, too."

"So what if they try out? You're a natural teacher. You can get the part if you just stay calm and be natural."

"I'm not good at being natural," Heather said. "I get a little . . ."

"Stiff?"

"Yeah, how'd you know?"

"I don't know. I just took a guess." I just couldn't bring myself to tell her that she's so stiff she makes a flagpole seem wiggly. Frankie and Ashley and I have always commented that Heather Payne looks like she's got her braids pulled too tight.

"Maybe you could teach me to relax?" Heather said, almost in a whisper. I think she was blushing, somewhere between her eyebrows and her braids. Asking for help didn't come easy for her, I could tell.

How could I teach her to relax? Man, that was almost as hard as teaching me math.

"My friend Frankie always tells me that oxygen is power," I said to her.

"Oxygen is a molecule," Heather said.

"Yeah, but his mom, who's a yoga teacher, taught him to use those molecules to relax. It's a deep-breathing technique. He taught me and I can teach you, if you like."

Heather just nodded. This was getting weird.

We were acting almost like . . . well . . . almost like friends.

"First you take a deep breath in," I said, "and as you do, you say 'I am' in your mind."

I took a deep breath in, to demonstrate. Heather did, too.

"Then you let the breath out, and as you do, you say 'relaxed' in your mind while you push the air out. Try it."

Heather blew out a big breath, and I could see her lips moving, saying the word "relaxed."

"How's it feel?" I asked her.

"I feel a little light-headed."

"Cool," I said. "That's the first stop on the road to relaxation."

The bell for school rang, and we had to hurry to put the rest of the books back on the shelf. As we quickly stacked them, I saw Heather practicing her relaxation breathing. Suddenly, she looked over at me and smiled.

"You know what, Hank?" she said. "I have the feeling that my braids are pulled too tight, if you know what I mean."

Did I ever!

I couldn't wait to tell Frankie. Apparently, that yoga breathing is some mighty powerful stuff.

CHAPTER 11

I SPENT THE REST OF THAT DAY secretly warming up for the audition, getting into the character of the king. To other people, it might have just looked like I was acting weird. Like when Ms. Adolf asked me to take the attendance records to the office, I bowed and said, "Madame, the record of my subjects shall remain safe inside my kingly robes," which by the way was actually my grey hooded Mets sweatshirt. At lunch, when I picked up my macaroni and cheese from the cafeteria line, I asked Frankie to taste it first, to make sure no one was trying to poison the king. Wouldn't you know, he kept tasting it and tasting it until he ate it all. I tell you, you could go hungry being king.

When the final bell of the day rang, I shot out of my seat and headed for the door. The auditions were in the multipurpose room, and I wanted to be the first one to sign up for the part of the king.

"Your backpack, Henry," Ms. Adolf said, tapping me on the shoulder. "I notice it's not on your back, which is where a backpack should reside."

"I got it, dude," Frankie said, taking the backpack from her as he swung down the aisle and headed for the door. "The king shouldn't have to carry his own stuff."

That Frankie. He is such a great friend. He'll support me no matter what I want to do.

As we headed down the stairs to the multi-purpose room, a bad smell came up behind us. It smelled like rotten lettuce mixed with soggy newspapers. And if you're wondering how I could possibly know what that particular combo smells like, then you haven't been around the bottom of Katherine's cage the day before Emily cleans it. Katherine is my sister's pet iguana, and aside from being one ugly creature, she is also one smelly creature. Other than Katherine, only one animal on the planet could possibly smell like that, and this one wore sneakers the size of battleships as they pounded behind me on the stairway.

"Shove over, Zipperbutt, and let the real king

pass," Nick McKelty said, blasting some of his iguana-cage breath my way.

"McKelty, the only kingdom you rule is Gross Land," Ashley said. "Don't you ever brush your teeth?"

"I have people who do that for me," McKelty snarled. It seemed like he was rehearsing for the part of the king, too.

"Well, dude, they must be on vacation," Frankie said.

"As king, I have granted them a few days off," McKelty said. Uh-oh, he seemed pretty into this king thing. I was going to have some competition.

"Give it up, McKelty," Ashley said. "You won't get the part. You wouldn't know a king if you fell on one."

"For your information, my great-great-grandfather on my mother's side was the King of Albania," McKelty lied, as usual. He had the McKelty factor, which is truth times a hundred, working overtime.

"His reign only lasted six hours because he was bitten on his butt by a black widow spider as he rode his horse to a duel," McKelty went on. "But he's a huge legend in Albania."

"He's a legend in your mind," Ashley said.

"Which, by the way, dude, has nothing huge about it," Frankie added.

We all cracked up.

"You're laughing now, Zippertoes," McKelty said, "but you won't be laughing when I get the part of the king."

He let out another blast of iguana-cage breath and blew past us. People clear the way when they smell him coming.

There was a long line of kids waiting outside the multipurpose room. There were clipboards laid out on a table, with the name of each role written in thick black letters at the top. You were supposed to put your name down for the part you wanted to audition for. There was one clipboard that said PRODUCTION STAFF. Frankie and Ashley headed for that list. Ashley signed up to be the costume designer, and Frankie put his name down for stage manager.

I picked up the KING clipboard, and of course, the first name on the list was Nick McKelty. I was surprised to see that a bunch of other guys had signed up to audition, too, including Luke Whitman. If he were a king, I guess he'd have to command one of his unlucky subjects to pick his nose for him. What a job, to be the royal nose picker.

As I was signing my name, I glanced over at the clipboard that said ANNA on top. Katie Sperling was the first one to sign up. Man, wouldn't that be great if she got the part and I got to play the king? I mean, I'd get to dance with her, and here's the best part—she couldn't say no when I asked her.

Then I saw Heather standing at the back of the line. She was just hanging out around the edge of the crowd of kids, not pushing her way to the table to get to the clipboards like the rest of us were.

"Come on, Heather," I called out to her. "Put your name down."

"I've changed my mind. I'm not sure I have the time."

"What are you talking about? You want to play Anna."

"But what happens if I don't get the part?" she said, so softly I could barely hear her over the noise of all the kids shouting in the hall.

"You'll never know unless you try," I said, picking up the clipboard and shoving it her way.

She took it, but I didn't see whether she signed up or not, because just then, the doors opened and Devore stepped out into the hall.

"Good afternoon, fellow theater lovers," he said, flinging his cape around like Superman. "Allow me to invite you into the magical world of drama."

He turned on his heel and floated into the multipurpose room. There was a platform set up at the far end, and chairs set up in a semicircle around it. Mrs. Crock was sitting on the platform with a yellow pad and a Sharpie. She looked really happy to be his assistant. We all took our seats in the chairs as Devore took his place on the platform.

"Let me remind you that you must be respectful while each of your friends is auditioning," he said. "The creative spirit needs silence to flourish."

Luke Whitman made a farting noise with his mouth. Devore stared at him.

"What part are you trying out for, young man?"

"The king," Luke answered.

"I do not recall the king communicating with the use of body sounds," Devore said. "However, if that is your particular talent, perhaps you should try out for the role of elephant boy. Body sounds are definitely in character there."

"I assure you, Luke has lots of body sounds, Mr. Devore," Mrs. Crock said. "I mean, Simply Devore."

Devore clapped his hands to get our attention.

"The first part we will be casting today is that of the king," he said.

Great. I'm ready to audition. Bring it on, Devore.

"We have five young men who have signed up for the part. Ryan Shimozato. Hank Zipzer. Nick McKelty. Luke Whitman. And Salvatore Mendez."

Okay, that's the competition, Hankster. It's good to know the competition.

"For purposes of the audition, Mrs. Crock will play Anna."

That's good. Mrs. Crock and I get along great. We've bonded over her lunch salad many times while I was waiting to see Principal Love.

"Now, who would like to read first?"

My hand shot up. Only then did my brain actually hear the words. When the word *read* reached my brain, my hand shot down.

"Did he say read?" I whispered to Frankie and Ashley.

"It's an audition," Ashley said. "You have to read the lines from the script."

"But I thought I was just supposed to pretend to be the king," I said. "I've been working on that since yesterday."

"It's a play, dude," Frankie said. "There's an actual script involved."

I can't read out loud without practicing first. Hey, I can't read quietly. Face it. Reading and I don't get along.

It was a scene between the king and Anna, where Anna tries to teach the king to dance, but he doesn't want to learn, because he's the king and he thinks he knows everything. Salvatore Mendez went first. He's from Puerto Rico, and when he read the lines, he did it with a little Spanish accent. He was good, and I could tell he really wanted the part, because at the end of the scene, he even kissed Mrs. Crock's hand. That's wanting the part, all right.

Luke Whitman went next. He tried to kiss Mrs. Crock's hand, too, but she wouldn't let him. Everyone in the school knows that wherever Luke Whitman's lips have been is some-place you don't want to be. Too bad he wasn't trying out for King of Cootyland, which he'd be a natural for.

While Ryan Shimozato was auditioning, I tried to say the lines silently while he said them out loud. It was a lot to memorize, but that was my only hope.

If you have to read, Hankster, you're a dead duck. Not in front of everyone. Not as slowly as you do. Not out loud.

Ryan Shimozato looked good as the king, but even I could tell he was no actor. He read the lines like he was reading his earth science textbook, which happens to be his best subject.

"We have two actors left," Devore said. "Mr. Nick McKelty and Mr. Hank Zipzer. Mr. Zipzer, are you ready to take the stage?"

No, I'm not! I haven't memorized all the lines yet!

"Much as I'd like to go next, Simply Devore, and I do appreciate your calling on me, I think I'll let McKelty go next," I said. "I'm sure there's so much I can learn from watching him audi-tion."

Yeah, like the lines!

"I like your attitude, Mr. Zipzer," Devore said. "There is so much one actor can learn from another."

"There's a lot you can learn from me," McKelty said, wedging his thick body out of his seat. "Pay attention while I show you how this theater thing is done."

"Humility, Mr. McKelty," Devore said.

"I got that, too," McKelty said, as if he even knew what the word meant. To be honest, I didn't know what it meant, either, so I shouldn't talk.

I don't know if McKelty was any good, but he was certainly loud. I'll bet you could hear him all the way to Mr. Kim's grocery store on the corner of 78th and Amsterdam. He paced around with his hands on his hips, yelling and blasting his iguana-cage breath right in poor Mrs. Crock's face. At one point, a glob of McKelty spit left his mouth and landed squarely on the tip of Mrs. Crock's nose. I think Mrs. Crock almost passed out, but she was a trooper and hung in there, smiling to the bitter end.

When McKelty was finished with the scene, he applauded himself. Devore nodded his head and wrote a lot of comments on his yellow pad.

"Thank you for your excellent effort," he said.

"See, I knew I'd get the part," McKelty said as he took his seat back in the semicircle. "You'll never top that, Zipzer."

I stood up and went to the platform. Mrs. Crock flashed me a reassuring smile as she handed me the script.

"You'll do fine, Hank," she whispered. I think she was just glad to be out of the line of bad breath and spitfire. Then she read her first line, which I was supposed to answer.

"Your highness," she said. "I think it's time you learned to dance. Have you ever danced before?"

I looked down at the script for the answer, but the words started to blur right before my eyes. I had a choice. I could either panic, or do what I did.

I put my hands on my hips, pulled myself up to my full height, which isn't that high, but is the best I've got. I looked Mrs. Crock right in the eye and spoke.

"Behold these feet," I said. "They are kingly feet, and they know everything his highness needs to know."

That line was not in the script, but good old Mrs. Crock answered me, anyway.

"But your highness does not know how to dance," Mrs. Crock said.

"Are you questioning me?" I shouted. "Do my ears hear a question?"

Mrs. Crock didn't answer. This line was nothing like the script, and obviously I had lost her completely. I had no choice but to take over.

"I shall dance when the spirit moves me," I said. "As a matter of fact, I feel the impulse speeding to my feet now. They are calling me to dance."

With that, I grabbed Mrs. Crock around her waist, took her hand in mine, and twirled her around in a circle. I happen to know quite a few fancy turns, because last year, when my mom decided to take ballroom dancing lessons with my dad, he refused to practice, so I became her partner when she went over the steps on the living room rug. And you'd never guess it, but old Mrs. Crock was pretty light on her feet herself. We twirled around until I got so dizzy I nearly passed out.

I let Mrs. Crock go and raised my arms in a kingly way.

"I believe that ends the discussion about dancing," I proclaimed. "The king's royal feet need to nap now."

I threw a kingly glance over at Devore and marched off the stage. Out of the corner of my eye, all I could see was that Devore's mouth was hanging open so far, his jaw was nearly touching the ground.

CHAPTER 12

DEVORE HAD TOLD US not to expect to hear about the audition results until everyone had finished. He said we had to watch everyone's audition out of respect for the performer.

Katie Sperling was the first to audition for Anna. I was happy to watch her, out of respect for the performer, naturally. Also out of respect for the fact that she is one beautiful fifth-grader.

Katie really did look the part of Anna. She had put on a sparkly blouse and a long sparkly skirt. When you looked at her, you believed that this was someone the King of Siam was going to fall madly in love with. But the problem with Katie came when she read her lines. After each line, she giggled. So it went like this:

KING: You are to be the governess to my children?

KATIE: Yes, your highness. *Giggle, giggle, giggle.*

KING: And as part of your job, you are expecting to teach me to dance?

KATIE: It would set an example . . . *giggle, giggle, giggle* . . . for the . . . *giggle, giggle, giggle* . . . children. *Louder giggle, followed by collapsing on the stage in giggles.*

Devore stopped the scene after that line.

"Tell me, young lady," he said to Katie. "Do you think it is possible for you to say one line without finding it so amusing?"

"Sure," Katie said with a giggle. Then she looked over at her best friend, Kim Paulson. Kim started to laugh so hard she had to leave the room. With that, Katie lost it completely and burst out laughing, too, right in Devore's face.

"Is someone tickling your ear with a feather?" Devore asked her.

"I'll get serious now," she said. "I promise."

With that, she exploded in such a giggle fit that she got tears in her eyes and ran off the stage, following Kim out of the door.

I guess Heather had finally decided to sign up, because Devore called her name next. She couldn't have been more opposite than Katie Sperling. There was no giggling, which as you know by now, there usually isn't when Heather

Payne is involved. Unlike me, she had memorized every word on the page, so when she got up to read her part, it was like she was reciting a poem at a graduation ceremony. She said each word, one-at-a-time. She was stiff as a wooden puppet.

Devore was playing the king, and I'm sure that was plenty scary. He had one of those Darth Vader voices that fills your ears with nothing but its sound.

"Miss Anna," he bellowed. "I will not dance. I am the King of Siam. I do not dance with lowly teachers."

"Are you afraid? Perhaps you might enjoy it, sire," Heather said in a robotlike voice.

She sounded like enjoying anything was the furthest thing from her mind. In fact, she was giving a good impression of someone on the verge of throwing up. She needed to relax. This was going nowhere.

Oddly enough, I felt sorry for Heather. I wanted to help her.

Silently, I stood up from the semicircle of chairs and tiptoed over to the platform until I was directly behind Devore. He was such a large man, it was easy for someone my size to hide behind him. I peeked out from behind his cape and tried to get Heather's attention.

Heather's eyes darted from Devore to me.

"*I am relaxed,*" I mouthed to her, and then went on to demonstrate my best yoga deep-breathing technique. Devore whipped around and saw me.

"What exactly are you doing, Mr. Zipzer?" he asked.

I looked past Devore, locking straight into Heather's eyes.

"I am *relaxing*!" I said right to her. "*If you know what I mean.*" Then I let out a big old yoga breath.

"Perhaps you could relax in the hall, Mr. Zipzer," he said. "Not in the middle of this young lady's audition."

"You're absolutely right, Devore," I said. "I'll wait to *relax* until Heather has finished her audition in a *relaxing* kind of way. Because we all enjoy breathing *in* and *out* in situations that are too tense to be *relaxed* in."

Devore's attention was on me, but out of the corner of my eye, I saw that Heather had gotten my point. She was yoga-breathing her brains out, mouthing the words "I am relaxed" just like I had shown her. Her cheeks had turned pink, and I swear, her braids seemed to be loosening up around her face. She didn't look like a person on the verge of throwing up any longer.

"And now if you will leave the stage," Devore said, gesturing me off with his big black cape. He turned to Heather and said, "I hope this hasn't broken your concentration."

"Oh, no," she said, breathing in and out deeply. "I am relaxed!"

Way to go, Heather Payne.

"Where were we?" Devore said. "Ah, yes, I was telling you that the king does not dance with lowly teachers."

"Well, if you're truly not afraid, then you will dance with me," Heather said, talking in a natural rhythm, with even a little smile in her voice. "May I have this dance, your highness?"

Then she extended her hand to Devore. Wow. That was brave. And it was good. I mean, she looked shy, but comfortable, in a teacher kind of way. I found myself thinking that if I were the king, I would dance with her.

Wait a minute, Hank. Are you actually saying you would really rather dance with Heather Payne than Katie Sperling?

I couldn't believe what was going on inside my brain. I mean, that morning I had been one kind of person, the kind of person who would have given up my weekend TV privileges to dance with Katie Sperling. And by afternoon, I was a completely other person, the kind of person who actually would have liked to dance with Heather Payne. The girl whose braids were pulled too tight. The girl with math on the mind.

Boy, life is strange.

CHAPTER 13

AFTER EVERYONE HAD AUDITIONED, Devore huddled with Mrs. Crock, going over lots of notes he had made on the yellow pad on his clipboard. While we were waiting, McKelty looked over at me and whispered, "I got it."

I just stared at him. Could he be right? I mean, how could Godzilla play the king? Well, maybe he could. After all, McKelty is tall. And maybe kings are supposed to be tall. What if there's a height requirement for the king? I never thought of that.

"I am so much better at this than you are," McKelty continued, moving over to the empty chair next to me.

"Let's just wait and see if Devore agrees with you," I said halfheartedly.

"I've been thinking about it, Zipperbutt," McKelty said. "And I have the perfect role for you. You can sweep the stage. I don't want my bare feet to get dirty."

"Why not? Then they'd match your face. Looks like you never wash that."

Devore stood up and came to the front of the platform. We all got really quiet. This was it. I closed my eyes. I clenched my fists. I could feel every muscle tighten up. The only thing loose on my body was my ear drum, so I could hear what he was going to say.

"Let me begin by congratulating all of you," Devore said. "Each and every one of you brought a delightful quality to your readings. And therefore, there will be a part for each of you in the play."

"Yeah, *Hank*erchief here volunteered to sweep the floors," McKelty shouted out, poking me in the ribs.

"Unfortunately, he won't have the time to do that," Devore said. "Because after much deliberation, I have chosen Hank Zipzer to play the role of the King of Siam."

He said my name! There it was floating out in the air for everyone to hear. Hank Zipzer will play the role of the King of Siam!

Ashley and Frankie jumped up to high-five me, but I couldn't move a muscle. I was frozen in my seat. The news stunned me. The only thing that moved was my lips, and they were smiling.

I hadn't said one line the way it was written.

I hadn't memorized one word.

And yes, I am short.

And yet, he called my name.

Like Papa Pete always says, if you have the will, there is a way. And man oh man, did I have the will! And did I ever find the way!

Suddenly, I noticed Nick McKelty staring at me, with all three of his eyes.

"Now I know for sure," McKelty said. "Devore must be blind and deaf."

"It's okay, Nick," I said. "You'll have a part. And I promise, I'll help you find that broom."

The room was still buzzing, but Devore quieted everyone down.

"Settle, people," he said. "I have another announcement to make. Let me introduce you to your new Anna."

We all got instantly quiet, except for Katie Sperling, who giggled. I looked over at Heather. She looked like she was going to hurl her peanut butter and jelly. I knew the feeling. I had just been there one minute before.

"Miss Heather Payne will play Anna," Devore

said. "And I'm sure, brilliantly. Congratulations, young lady."

The room went totally quiet. And then, the weirdest thing happened. Heather Payne stood up, pumped her fist about twenty times, and then yelped like a rhino celebrating her first birthday. Actually, I don't know if rhinos yelp or even make any sound at all. But if they did, I'm sure it would be as loud and as wild as that sound that Heather Payne made.

This was an amazing sight. No one had ever seen Heather Payne lose control before. Well, maybe that time in first grade when she discovered that the square root of nine was three. She got really excited and twirled around so fast her braids looked like a pinwheel at the county fair. But this whooping thing had us all really surprised.

After the yelping ended, Heather looked pretty shocked herself.

"Oh . . . I'm sorry," she said, and immediately sat down.

"No need to apologize, young lady," Devore said. "The creative spirit set free is a pleasure to behold."

Nick McKelty stood up and started to leave.

"Where are you going, young man?" Devore asked. "I haven't finished the announcements or dismissed the class."

"I'm out of here," McKelty said. "This whole play thing sucks."

"Before you leave, consider this," Devore said. "I have chosen you to be the understudy."

The understudy? I had never heard that word before, but it described me better than it did Nick. I mean, I under-study for everything. Like math, spelling, science. In fact, I took a science test on the evaporation cycle without even reading the chapter. That's what I call understudying.

"What's an understudy?" Ashley asked. Ashley is one of those smart kids who isn't afraid to ask a question. Me, I'm always afraid to show what I don't know, because I assume everyone else knows more than I do.

"An understudy is the person who gets to play the part should the lead actor not be able to," Devore explained.

"So, like, if Zipperbutt here gets a stomachache and can't go on, then I'll get to be the king," McKelty said. Boy, he was quick to catch on, that guy.

"Precisely, Nick," Devore said. "Being an understudy is a very important job."

"Then I'll take it," McKelty said. "I was made for important jobs."

"Excellent," Devore said. "I will post all the crew positions tomorrow. Check the board, people, and report for rehearsals after school."

As we started out, everyone was congratulating me and wishing me luck.

"And one more thing," Devore called after us. "In the theater, it is bad luck to wish someone good luck. We simply say, break a leg. So break a leg, everyone."

McKelty looked over at me.

"Especially you, Zipperbutt. Break a leg. While you're at it, break two."

CHAPTER 14

"I GOT IT!" I screamed, bursting into our apartment after school.

My dad was sitting at the dining room table as usual, staring at his computer screen, which was filled with so many numbers and charts that it looked like a page in a math book. He pushed his glasses up on top of his head and stared at me.

"What did you get, Hank? I'm hoping it's a good grade."

"Better than that!" I smiled at him, barely able to hold the secret. "Mom! I have some great news!"

I wanted to tell them both at once. I knew my mom was home and in the kitchen, because I could smell dinner cooking. I couldn't identify it, but I could smell it. It smelled . . . well . . . not good, but interesting.

My mom came through the swinging door from the kitchen, wiping her hands on a dish towel. Her blond hair had chunks of food hanging off it, which happens when she's really absorbed in her cooking. I hoped that it might be chunks of something delicious like pot roast or potato salad, like she makes for our family deli, the Crunchy Pickle. But the things hanging off her hair looked like little white worms. They were pale and squiggly, two things that you definitely don't want your dinner to be.

"Get your ears ready to hear something really cool, you guys," I said.

"My ears can hardly wait." My mom laughed.

But my dad just said, "Enough with the drama, Hank. Say what you have to say."

"Well," I said, taking a deep bow. "You are now looking at the new King of Siam. I grant you the right to ask me any question you'd like."

"Do I get to make the costume?" my mom asked, clapping her hands with excitement. "I can see you now in flowing gold pantaloons and a sequined vest."

"No offense, Mom, but we might have to lighten up on the sequins. Sparkly clothes aren't exactly my look."

"Maybe I'll sew a Mets emblem on the back of your vest," she suggested, which shows you just how cool my mom really is. "You'd have to add something about baseball in the script, of course, to make it seem—"

"Randi," my dad interrupted, in his interrupting voice. "Let's not put the cart before the horse. Hank and I have a deal that if he doesn't get a B-plus on his math test, there will be no need for a sequined vest or any other kingly clothes."

"No problemo, Dad. The math test is cool. I got that all covered."

"When have I heard that before?"

"Really, Dad. I'm going to work so hard with Heather Payne. Just this morning, we had an eye-opening long division session."

"I hear Heather Payne got the part of Anna," Emily said, as she strolled into the living room with her iguana, Katherine, riding on her shoulder.

"You heard right," I said. "So now she's tutoring me in real life *and* in the play. How funny is that!"

"I've got an idea!" my mom said. "Let's have her over for dinner!"

"Wow-ee. Whoa-ee. Let's slow it down, Mom. I mean, Heather and I are just barely getting to know each other."

"I know that tone of voice," Emily said in a singsong voice. "Sounds like somebody has a crush on somebody."

"Wow-ee. Whoa-ee. Let's slow it down, Em. I mean, the Zipzer women are out of control here."

"Kathy," Emily said, talking to Katherine but aiming her comment directly toward me. "Wouldn't it be great if Heather Payne became Hank's girlfriend? I admire her ability to excel in school."

"Of course you do," I answered. "That's because good grades are all you ever think about."

"It wouldn't hurt you to spend some time thinking about that very subject," my dad said, right on cue like I knew he would.

"Just think of it," Emily said. "Heather and I could do interclass research projects together. I wonder if she's interested in the life cycle of reptiles."

"Emily, you are a fountain of fun ideas," I said. "As a matter of fact, 'fun' should be your middle name. Mom, is there any way of changing Emily *Daphne* Zipzer to Emily *Fun* Zipzer? Legally, I mean?"

My mom laughed. True, she's an easy person to make laugh, but still, I like it that she thinks I'm funny.

"Let's make dinner a celebration of the good news," she said. "I'm trying out a brand-new recipe—pureed dehydrated prunes over a bed of alfalfa and broccoli sprouts."

Ah, at least now I knew what was in her hair. I didn't like it any better, but I could identify those wormy thingies.

It was going to take another half an hour for all that pruney mess to get itself on a plate, so I went to my room and got busy. Devore had given me the script and told me to underline all the king's lines in yellow highlighter. That way, I'd know which lines I was supposed to read in rehearsal.

I sat down at my desk and got to work with the highlighter. I didn't have any problem finding my lines. Every time I saw the word *king*, I just highlighted all the words that followed it. I was super-concentrating, which I can do when I'm really interested in something. I never looked up, and after I had gone through the whole script, I sat back and flipped through the pages.

Wow-ee. Whoa-ee. That was a lot of yellow!

As I sat there wondering how I was ever going to read all those lines, let alone memorize them, there was a knock on my bedroom door.

"Enter," I called out, trying out my kingly voice.

Emily came in, with Katherine the Ugly riding on her shoulder.

"You've not asked your ruler's permission to enter with a lizoid," I bellowed.

"First of all, Hank, there is no such thing as a lizoid. And second of all, Kathy and I came to help, but if you don't want it, we can leave."

Emily turned to go, and Katherine threw me a parting hiss.

"Wait a sec," I said. "Help with what?"

"I think we both know that you're going to need a lot of help learning your lines." Emily's voice was quiet, like she was sharing a secret with me.

"Why would you say that?"

"First, because reading is hard for you. And

second, because reading is hard for you."

"What's third?" I snapped back, which wasn't fair, because I think Emily was truly trying to help. It's hard for me to accept help, especially from my younger sister, even though I knew she had a point.

"Okay, maybe we could read one scene together," I said. "If you promise to dump the iguana. I don't rehearse with lizoids. Sorry. I mean, lizards."

"Katherine and I are a team," Emily said. "We rehearse together or not at all."

She drives a hard bargain, that Emily. But I looked down at all that yellow highlighting and knew I could use the help.

"Okay," I said. "Katherine stays. Just tell her to breathe in the other direction. I don't want her iguana breath in my face."

Emily stood right next to me, so we could read from the script together. Luckily for my nose, she did move Katherine to her other shoulder. Emily read Anna's line, and I read the king's. Or at least, I tried to.

"Welcome to my palace," I said. "And to my . . . my . . ."

The word started with an *r*, and looked like

really or *real*, but it wasn't either of those.

"Realm," Emily whispered. "It's another word for kingdom."

"Of course it is," I snapped.

I guess Katherine didn't like my tone of voice, because she hissed at me and shot out her sticky grey tongue real close to my face region.

Or maybe she was just upset that she didn't have a line.

Tough luck, Kath. I'm the king and you're the iguana.

"Your highness, it is my honor to serve as the governess to your children," Emily read. My turn.

"Let me in . . . in . . . in . . . something you to them now."

"Introduce," Emily whispered again. "Just take the time to sound it out."

"Introduce," I repeated. And I made a mental note to remember that word.

"I am eager to meet the children," Emily read, and then she turned to Katherine. "Aren't we, Kathy?"

"Wait a minute," I objected. "I may not be a great reader, but I know that's not in the script for sure."

"Hank, Kathy needs a line. She's an actor, too."

Katherine lifted her upper lip, or whatever you call that flap of scaly skin above her mouth, and showed what looked like all 188 of her yellowish teeth. Boy, could she use a good brushing.

Good grief, I think she's smiling. What a ham!

"Enough of that, Katherine," I said. "You're hogging the show."

"She's improvising," Emily said.

"Well, tell her to read the script and notice that she's not in it."

Katherine hissed at me again, this time with so much force that I actually fell backward from her hot iguana breath on my face.

"And while you're at it, you could buy yourself a new toothbrush," I said to her.

We went on rehearsing until dinnertime. I'd read a line. Emily would correct it. Emily would read her line. And Katherine would hiss. Line. Correction. Line. Hiss. Line. Correction. Line. Hiss.

It was a pretty unusual way to rehearse, I'll give you that. But by the time we sat down to alfalfa and broccoli sprouts in prune sauce, I had made it through the entire first scene and had memorized most of the lines.

Let me give you two pieces of advice. First, if you're ever in the school play, it really helps to read your lines out loud. And second, if you ever have a chance to act with an iguana, don't.

CHAPTER 15

HEATHER AND I WORKED TOGETHER on long division every single morning before school. I'm not going to tell you a lot about our peer tutoring sessions, because they were filled with words that made me dizzy to say, let alone write down. Words like "divisor" and "dividend" and "quotient" and "remainder." Whoa . . . I better stop, because I'm getting dizzy right now.

I will tell you two things, though, about our peer tutoring sessions.

First, by the middle of the second week, I actually started to get the long division problems right most of the time.

Next, and almost as surprising, I began to like Heather Payne.

Yes, you heard me. I, Henry Daniel Zipzer, started to like Heather Huffington Payne. (Don't even ask about the Huffington. It's a long story involving her grandmother and the birdseed salesman she fell in love with.)

I found out some things about Heather I never would have dreamed of in a million trillion years. Like that she's a Mets fan, just like me. And that she licks the icing off her Ding Dongs before eating the cake, just like me. And that when she laughs too hard, she gets the hiccups. I taught her my special Hank Zipzer hiccup cure where you swallow water and cover your ears at the same time, and it seemed to work.

Every day after school, we went to rehearsals. Heather knew all her lines from the first day. I learned mine, then forgot them, learned them, and forgot them again.

"Hank, I implore you to study your lines," Devore said to me every single day. I did study my lines. It's just that I have a nonstick kind of brain.

The good thing is that when I'd mess up on a line, I'd always come up with something else to say. Devore called that improvising, which means making up a line on the spot. Heather hated it when I improvised. She'd just stand there, trying to improvise an answer. But if it wasn't in the script, she couldn't come up with anything.

"Heather, you must try to go with the flow," Devore told her. "Listen to your fellow actor, and respond. Be free, like Hank is."

"I'll try," she said.

"You must do more than try," Devore explained. "Unexpected things happen on stage, but the show must always go on. Improvising is the key."

But Heather was as stiff as a board. The non-improviser of all non-improvisers.

One day, we were rehearsing the opening scene, where Anna arrives in Siam and is being introduced to the king. I was supposed to welcome her to my palace. Then I was supposed to comment on what a long and tiring journey she'd had. Then Luke Whitman, playing the elephant boy, was supposed to take her suitcase and help her to her room.

"Welcome to my palace," I said, as we began the scene.

"Thank you, your highness," she answered. Then she waited. And waited. And waited. I had completely forgotten my line about her tiring journey. Finally, I just said whatever came to my mind.

"We are happy to have you here in Siam," I said, "the land of wild elephants and spicy food."

"Huh?" Heather answered.

"Improvise, my dear," Devore whispered from the wings. But she couldn't.

"Ah, Siam," I continued, "the land where we eat rice from the earth and eels from the river."

"Eeeuuuwww," Heather said.

"Go with the flow," Devore whispered. But she couldn't.

"I have ruled this land and its people since I was a child, and now I have nineteen children of my own," I said.

"Ahh," Heather answered.

"Mr. Whitman, help her," Devore called from the sidelines.

"Come on, Anna. I'll take you to see the elephants," Luke said, grabbing Heather's hand and yanking her off the stage. They bumped smack into Nick McKelty, who was snickering in the wings.

"You suck," McKelty said to Heather, in a really loud voice. "You totally stink up the place."

Devore picked up the broom and marched right up to McKelty.

"Sweep," he said. "And when you're finished, sweep some more."

I went over to Heather, who was sitting on the king's throne, crumpled up in a ball. I knew this was really embarrassing for her. She can do everything perfectly. And Luke Whitman can't do anything perfectly, except pick his nose and scratch his mosquito bites. Yet here *he* was, helping *her*.

"McKelty's right," she said to me. "I do suck."

"You'll get the hang of it," I said. "You just have to relax, if you know what I mean."

"That's just it, Hank. I don't know what you mean. I know what the word 'relax' means, but I don't know how to do it."

"Like when people tell me to focus." I nodded. "I know what the word means, but I don't have a clue how to do it."

I knew Heather was feeling frustrated, because I am the world's greatest expert in feeling frustrated. What she needed was a little encouragement.

"You know what I think?" I said. "I think one day, you'll open your mouth and Anna will come out. Just like you're her and she's you."

"Thanks for believing in me, Hank," she said.

"Besides, you're a great peer tutor," I went on. "Just ask me anything about long division."

"Okay, what's one hundred divided by ten?"

"I forget."

"What?" she shrieked.

"Just kidding, teach. Honest. It's ten. There, are you happy?"

"Yes," she said. "I am."

CHAPTER 16

EVEN THOUGH HE CONTINUED to be totally obnoxious, McKelty attended every single rehearsal. Devore insisted on it because being the understudy for the king was a very important job.

"Why do I have to stay?" McKelty complained during the second week, jelly from his donut dripping down his chin. "It's boring to watch Zipperfoot tromp around on the stage."

"You never know when you'll be called upon to step in," Devore said to McKelty. "Something could befall the lead actor, and he won't be able to show up for a performance. So you have to know every word and every move."

I could see a light go on in McKelty's eyes. And I thought a saw a little puff of smoke come out of his ears. That meant he was thinking.

"So, like, if Hank gets, like, say, a bad cold or lost in the fog or, like, is in a major shipwreck or . . ."

Or gets anything less than a B-plus on my math test, I thought.

"So, like, that's when I get to take my rightful place on the throne," McKelty said, proud that he had finished his thought with a bang.

"Precisely," said Devore. He seemed a little surprised that McKelty was almost two weeks into rehearsal and only now understanding what an understudy did, but then, he didn't have the years of dealing with McKelty's thick head that the rest of us had.

That was all McKelty needed to hear to go into action. From then on, he was a one-man demolition derby, doing everything in his power to make sure that I wasn't able to play the part.

EIGHT TRULY ROTTEN THINGS McKELTY DID, EVEN THOUGH THERE WERE WAY MORE THAN TEN

1. He sneezed a big wet sneeze into a Kleenex and then stuffed the tissue into my jeans pocket so I'd have to touch it. No kidding. He really did that.
2. He kept trying to trip me coming down the

stairs, but his feet are so huge and he's so klutzy, he tripped himself instead.

3. He had his girlfriend, Joelle Atkins, call me on her cell phone, disguising her voice as Katie Sperling, and ask me to the movies the night of the play. I didn't fall for it, since Joelle sounds like Barney the Purple Dinosaur, and the one time I spoke to Katie Sperling on the phone in the second grade, she sounded like a movie star.

4. He told me Heather Payne had poison oak between her fingers, and if I danced with her, I'd get it and then it would spread all over my body and even behind my eyelids.

5. He tried to switch my milk carton at lunch with one that he had kept in his desk for several days, so I'd drink the sour milk and get a horrible stomachache. Luckily, my nose sniffed out the problem before the carton reached my mouth.

6. He locked me out of the multipurpose room before rehearsals. It's a good thing Devore saw my head bouncing around in the glass pane of the door as I frantically jumped up and down to see in. Fortunately, I was

wearing my basketball shoes, which make me jump higher.

7. He wrote a letter to Devore as if he were me, resigning from the play for "personal reasons." He's so stupid, though, he signed his own name.

8. He tried to convince Frankie and Ashley to talk me into resigning because he said the part should only be played by someone who is truly Siamese, and although he wasn't actually Siamese, he once petted a Siamese cat and didn't get an allergy attack, so he must be one-sixteenth Siamese.

It's funny, though, that McKelty was doing everything in his power to stop me from playing the king, when the one thing that could truly stop me was right there under his thick, hairy nose.

The unit test in long division.

CHAPTER 17

PAPA PETE ALWAYS SAYS that time flies when you're having fun. Well, I must have been having a ball, because those two and a half weeks until the math unit test flew by like a rocket in outer space. Between math tutoring in the morning and rehearsals in the afternoon, my days were full. I was so busy, I didn't even have time to get nervous about the test.

Until Friday, the second Friday in November, to be exact. The day of the unit test on long division. I woke up with a rumbling in my belly. It was like my stomach was talking to me, saying, "Hank Zipzer, can you do it? Can you pull off a B-plus?"

"Of course you can do it," Frankie said to me on our way to school. "Just stay calm and breathe. Remember, dude. Oxygen is power."

"And check your work," Ashley said. "No careless mistakes."

"Neatness counts," Emily chimed in. "Don't

be your usual sloppy self."

Heather and I didn't meet before school that day for tutoring. She said I knew the material cold, and she didn't want to make me nervous. So instead, I just hung out in the yard before school, watching the last of the fall leaves float to the ground and listening to my stomach rumble.

Ms. Adolf takes test days pretty seriously. Well, she takes every day pretty seriously, but on test days, she wouldn't crack a smile if two hundred clowns ran into class throwing whipped-cream pies and making funny faces.

"Hi, Ms. Adolf," I said as I walked past her desk that morning. I thought maybe if I smiled at her, she'd smile back. "Lovely day for a math test."

"Speak to me after the test, Henry," she said. "Then we'll see if you still think it's a lovely day."

Way to give a guy confidence, Ms. A.

Heather waved at me as she came in and took her seat. She flashed me a thumbs-up sign. She had total confidence in me.

I sure hope I live up to it.

The math test wasn't until after lunch, which

left me all day to worry about it. I kept busy, though. Between listening to my stomach rumble and biting my fingernails and yoga-breathing my head off, I had a lot to do.

I stopped by to visit Mr. Rock at lunch, and he told me how well he thought I was doing as the king. He'd been coming to rehearsals for the last week, because he was musical director and played the piano for our songs.

"You're a natural up there onstage," he said to me.

"Thanks," I said. "By the way, does seventy-two divided by six equal twelve?"

"I believe it does," he said. "Why?"

"No reason," I answered, as my stomach rumbled and I wandered out.

It was exactly one thirty when Ms. Adolf called an end to our silent reading period and told us to clear our desks.

"Put all your books away," she said. "Nothing but one sheet of paper and one pencil on your desk. If I find anything else, I will take it away."

She walked up and down each row, placing one test on each of our desks. When I first looked at the test, I had the same reaction I always have when I see a whole page of math problems. The numbers started to dance on the page, my mind went blank, and I got a little nauseous.

Oh, no you don't, Hankster. Not this time. Come on, now. Breathe and concentrate. You know this stuff.

Somehow, I managed to calm my mind and look at the test. There they were. Thirty-two nifty little long division problems, smiling up at me. I smiled back at them.

Hi, guys. How you doing? Let's make friends.

I looked over at Ms. Adolf, who was giving me an icy stare. I guess she had never seen anyone try to make friends with their math problems before. I wiped the smile off my face and got to work.

I didn't look up for one hour. At exactly two thirty, Ms. Adolf said, "Pencils down." I had just finished the very last problem.

I put my pencil down, and if I do say so myself, I was feeling pretty good about long division.

CHAPTER 18

DON'T ASK ME HOW I DID IT, but I managed to talk Ms. Adolf into grading my paper right away. I attached myself to the side of her desk like a barnacle on the bottom of a boat.

"Will you kindly back up, Henry?" she said. "You are sucking all the air out of my work space."

"Sorry, Ms. Adolf. I'm just a little anxious to see what I got."

"Breathing on your paper will not make it better," she said. "Why this sudden interest your mathematics performance?"

"I think my tutoring with Heather has really worked," I said. "I feel like long division and I have finally made friends."

"How pleasant for you," she said, picking up her red pencil. "Now if you'll allow me some air, I shall grade your paper."

Frankie had already told me that I had to get twenty-eight problems right to get a B-plus.

That meant I could miss four.

Before she even looked at my answers, Ms. Adolf took her red pencil and wrote "minus one" at the top of my paper.

"How could I have missed anything?" I asked her. "You haven't even gotten to my answers yet."

"You didn't write your full name and the date in the upper right-hand corner. That counts for one whole problem off."

"But, Ms. Adolf," I said, almost crying. "My initials are right there. H.Z."

"Remember Adolf's Rule Number Six?" she said. "Print your full name and the date legibly in the upper right-hand corner."

"You can't take a whole point off for that!" I whined.

"I can, and I did, Henry."

With that, she moved her red pencil over to the answer column and began to check my answers. I never took my eyes off that pencil as she moved it down my answers. I counted each red check. Number four was wrong. She paused at number seventeen, and I held my breath. Then came the red check. That was two problems wrong. Plus the name thing, so that's three.

She didn't make another check for a long time, and I could feel myself starting to smile.

You did it, Hank Zipzer. You aced this test!

But then came problem number twenty-seven. I never liked that number twenty-seven. It has an unlucky sound to it. And I missed it, all right. I felt my answer was pretty close to right, and I pointed that out to her.

"Shouldn't I get some credit for getting really close?" I asked.

"Mathematics is a precise science," Ms. Adolf said. "Now if you'll let me continue."

"Please do. But you're not going to find anything else wrong. Four wrong is my limit."

Four wrong was a B-plus. I knew I wasn't going to miss any more. I could just feel it.

Ms. Adolf's red pencil slid all the way down to the bottom of the answer column without making another check. Four wrong! Four wrong was a B-plus!

I started to jump up and down like a nutty kangaroo.

"Not so fast, Henry," Ms. Adolf said.

She placed her pencil on the very last answer of the test. And she put a big, fat red check next to it.

"No!" I said. "That problem couldn't be wrong. I remember going over it twice."

I pointed to my work on the test paper.

"See," I said. "Five hundred and sixty divided by twenty. It's twenty-eight. I figured it out. I know it's right. Look, I wrote twenty-eight right there on my paper."

Ms. Adolf pointed to the answer column.

"It says eighty-two here, Henry. Not twenty-eight."

"But I just flipped the number around when I transferred my work to the answer column. It happens."

"Once again, Henry, let me refer you to the word 'precision.' Right is right and wrong is wrong. And your answer is wrong."

She took her red pencil and moved it to the top of the test. MINUS FIVE, she wrote in big red letters. Eighty-four percent.

Eighty-four percent was a B.

"Ms. Adolf," I said, my heart pounding in my chest. "There's been a terrible mistake. I technically missed five, but if you look at it untechnically, I really and truly only missed four actual math questions!"

"In my book, it is still minus five," she said.

"But I'm supposed to get a B-plus. I have to get a B-plus."

"If I were giving you a grade in whining, you would certainly get a B-plus," Ms. Adolf said. "Perhaps even an A. But your grade on this math test is a B, Henry. And that's final."

"But . . ."

She took her red pencil and put a giant circle around the B at the top of my paper. Any other time I would have been thrilled to get a B. But when I looked at that big red grade on top of my test paper, all I wanted to do was rip it to shreds.

CHAPTER 19

FRANKIE AND ASHLEY WERE WAITING for me outside the front door of school.

"Dude," Frankie said. "Show me the B-plus."

I showed him the paper with the big, red B on the top.

"Okay, Zip. So that's a little lower than we had projected," Frankie said.

"But way better than you usually do," Ashley added.

"Good point, Ashweena. Listen, Zip, you've got to emphasize that to your dad," Frankie said. "This is *way* better than you usually do. Just keep hitting the 'way better' part. He'll come around."

I hoped he was right. All the way home, I hoped he was right. All the way into the lobby of our building, and up the elevator, I hoped he was right. As I got off the elevator and the doors closed, I heard Frankie repeating, "Remember,

Zip, the key word is 'way.' You did 'way better.'"

I put the key in the lock and took a few deep breaths in and out, repeating, "I am relaxed." And then, just to be truthful, I added, "Not really, but kind of."

My dad was working at the dining room table. I tried to determine if he was in a good mood or a bad mood. I thought I saw a few crumbs around his mouth and chin area, which was a good sign, because if he had recently eaten a piece of cinnamon crumb coffee cake with his afternoon cup of tea, that would have definitely put him in a good mood.

"Hey, Dad," I said, with a big smile in my voice.

He didn't look up. Uh-oh. That must've meant we were out of the cinnamon coffee cake and all we had were those two-day-old honey oat bran granola bars.

"So you'll never guess what happened today in school," I said, pulling up a chair and sitting down across the table from him.

"Is this about math, Hank?" he asked.

"Yes, it is," I said. "And it's good news."

For the first time, he took his fingers off the

keyboard and his eyes off the computer screen.

"You got your test back."

"That I did," I said. "Now, Dad, you know that I usually get a D or lower in math, especially a topic like long division, which can be very tricky."

"Cut to the chase, Hank."

"So, Dad, I am happy to tell you that I zoomed all the way up the grading scale. I did *way better* than I usually do."

"Hank, what did you get?"

I used the table as a drum, and I made a drumroll using the tips of my fingers. It sounded as much like "ta-da" as I could get it to.

"I got a big, gigantic, first-time-ever B! Can you believe it, Dad? I can't."

Okay, I'll admit there was a silence. A pretty long silence. But I didn't get discouraged because I thought he was probably thinking exactly how to congratulate me for my big improvement. So I stayed quiet and let him come up with the words himself.

"A B was not our agreement, Hank."

Oh, no. This wasn't going the way I had hoped. There was still time to turn it around.

"Dad, you have to admit, this is the best

I've ever done. This is huge. Frankie and Ashley were really excited. Even Ms. Adolf nodded her head at me. And in a positive way."

"You know the rule, Hank. My expectation was for you to get a B-plus. You agreed."

"But, Dad, she took points off just because I didn't transfer one of my answers correctly into the answer column. You have to admit, that's not math."

"That's work habits, Hank. And yours are half-baked, as usual."

"I'll do better next time, Dad. I'll bake my work habits until they're really well-done."

"Hank, a deal is a deal. As your father, my job is to set the standards and your job is to meet them. Period."

"No, Dad. That's not your job. Your job is to work at the computer and drive the van on family vacations and shout out all the right answers on *Jeopardy!* when we watch it together. That's a really important job, Dad."

"I've made a decision, Hank."

"Not about the play. Tell me it's not about the play. Is it?"

"You're going to have to go and tell the director that you can no longer participate."

At that very moment, my brain turned to cream cheese. I heard what my dad was saying, but it sounded like he was six million miles away, and his words were coming out of his mouth all slow and gooey, like the last little bit of maple syrup that hardens at the bottom of the bottle.

"Dad, they're counting on me. If I don't play the king, do you know who will? Nick McKelty, that's who. That's like putting pantaloons and a crown on a cow."

"Nick McKelty is not my concern," my dad said. "I am not doing this just to punish you, Hank. I'm doing this for your own good. Schoolwork comes first."

Schoolwork comes first.

Now that's a sentence I can honestly say I hate.

CHAPTER 2

AT RECESS THE NEXT DAY, I broke the news to Heather. I looked for her at tetherball, which is her favorite game, but she wasn't there. Finally, I found her pacing up and down along the back wall of the playground, which is a huge mural painted to look like the desert of Arizona.

"Hank," she said, "I'm so glad to see you. I'm having trouble with the scene where the king is disrespectful to Anna. And I'm still nervous about the dancing part . . ."

"Heather," I interrupted. "I can't be the king."

I thought it was best to just lay it out there. But she didn't get it.

"I understand," she said. "Just like I'm having trouble being Anna, which is why I thought we should rehearse this section before we show it to Devore."

"No, Heather. You're not understanding what I'm saying. I got a B on my math test, and my father is sticking to our agreement. I can't be the king."

"It's all my fault," she said. "I didn't do my job as your peer tutor."

"It's not you, Heather. I did better than I've ever done on a math test."

"So what happens with the play?" she said. Slowly, I could see the horrible realization dawn on her. "Oh, no. McKelty."

"Maybe he'll surprise us," I answered. But we both knew that the only surprising thing about Nick McKelty was how he could constantly break the world record for obnoxiousness.

If I thought telling Heather the news was hard, telling Devore was no picnic, either. I went to the multipurpose room after school and asked if I could have a word with him before rehearsal started. When I told him about my father's decision, he seemed stunned. I don't think anything like that had ever happened to him. I'm pretty sure people who act in off-Broadway shows don't get their acting privileges taken away by their dads.

"But surely your father knows the age-old rule of the theater world," he said, tossing his black cape over his shoulders. "The show must go on."

"My dad doesn't exactly live in the theater world," I tried to explain. "He lives more in the Do-As-I-Say-Or-You're-Grounded world."

"But doesn't he understand that your journey through the world is traveled on the river of the arts?"

"He gets seasick on rivers. Once he even threw up when we took a boat tour around Manhattan. He hurled right into the East River."

"I was speaking more of a poetic river," Devore said.

"He gets a little nauseous around poetry, too."

Devore paced back and forth, rubbing his goatee.

"The only solution is for me to call your father to discuss the matter," he said at last.

"That would only make my dad more angry," I said. "I made a deal, and I came close to holding up my end of it. But I didn't, and a deal's a deal."

I had to stop talking then, because I could feel the tears just on the other side of my eyeballs, waiting to flow down my cheeks. I turned away from Devore and took a seat in the folding chairs where only the understudies were sitting.

Devore took a deep breath, then clapped his hands and cleared his throat.

"Ladies and gentlemen of the cast and crew," he said. "I have a very important announcement. As of today, Mr. McKelty will play the part of the king."

You could hear everyone in the room groan in unison. From their places up on the stage, Frankie and Ashley looked over at me with such sad looks. I could tell they felt sorry for me, and to tell you the truth, it gets really old always being the one your friends have to feel sorry for.

The only one in the multipurpose room who didn't groan was you-know-who. When he heard the news, Nick McKelty shot out of his chair, pumped his fist like he had just hit a home run in the World Series, and did a victory dance so twitchy you could see his stomach jiggle under his shirt.

"Now you guys will see what a king really looks like," he shouted.

"Mr. McKelty, we don't have time for your shenanigans," Devore said. "Take your place on the stage."

McKelty clomped up to the stage, his big shoes making a loud echoing noise in the silent room.

"Places, everyone," Devore called.

But no one moved. Frankie was in the wings with his headset still around his neck. Ashley had stopped adjusting Heather's costume, and just stood there looking at me with tears in her eyes. Even Luke Whitman, as the elephant boy, actually took his finger out of his nose for a moment. That was a first.

"Mr. McKelty, I hope you've been watching very carefully these last two weeks, and paying attention to what Hank has been doing," Devore said. "An understudy must fit seamlessly into the production."

"Are you kidding? I'm not copying him," McKelty said. "I've been practicing my own style at home. You're not going to believe what you see."

"That's what I'm afraid of," I heard Devore whisper under his breath.

Mr. Rock had been sitting at the piano, watching everything unfold. I could feel him observing me, but I was glad he didn't say anything. Those tears were still there behind my eyeballs, and I wanted them to stay right where they were.

"Let's begin with the scene where Anna and the king dance for the first time," Devore said.

"Goody," McKelty said. "I'm a great dancer." Then he turned to Heather.

"Come on over here, pigtails. I'll give you a twirl around the stage like Zipzer could never do."

"Do I have to?" Heather asked Devore.

"I'm afraid so," Devore said. "Take your places. Mr. Rock, if you will."

Mr. Rock put his hands on the piano and played a big, fancy introduction. Frankie put on his headset, Ashley gave Heather a final fluff-up, and McKelty grunted like a wild boar. I guess it was his way of saying to Heather, "Shall we dance?"

He galumphed over to her and put his paw-like hand around her waist. With no warning, he grabbed her and started to spin in a circle. He twirled her so fast that she spun totally out of his grasp, careened across the stage like a top, bounced off Luke Whitman, bumped into at least four kindergartners playing the king's children, and landed in a heap on the throne, sideways, with her legs over the arm of the chair.

"Now that's how a king does it!" McKelty shouted, strutting across the stage like a peacock.

"Mr. McKelty, I suggest you control your enthusiasm before you throw your dance partner through the wall," Devore said.

Heather looked like she was going to cry.

I couldn't watch another second. I jumped to my feet and raced down the aisle, across the multipurpose room, through the double doors, and out into the hall.

I just stood there, hating my brain. For not remembering to put the date on my math test. *Come on, that is so simple.* For missing the first three easy problems. *Why didn't I check my work like Ashley said?* For not copying over the right answer on that last problem. *I should've gotten that right. I mean, I knew it.*

"Hank, you forgot this."

I turned around and there was Mr. Rock, holding my backpack. As usual, I had left it behind.

Is there anything I can do right? I can't even leave a room without forgetting something.

"Thanks, Mr. Rock," I said, taking the backpack from him. I turned to leave.

"Hank," he called after me. "If you really want to be in the play, there's got to be a way."

"It's not fair," I said, feeling all my frustration come rushing out at once. "And besides, you don't know my dad."

I let loose with the whole story and some of those tears, too. I wasn't embarrassed, though, because Mr. Rock is the kind of teacher you can say anything to. I don't know what I would do without him. He just listened to me talk, nodded, and then listened some more.

"Have you tried telling your feelings to your father?" he said, when I had finally come to the end of my words.

"Trust me, I did."

"Then you have to do it again," he said. "You're going to have to make yourself heard."

"Changing my father's mind about anything is impossible."

He nodded. We were both quiet. In the silence, we heard Nick McKelty's horrible, screeching voice blubbering through his lines.

We looked at each other and we both understood what I had to do.

CHAPTER 21

"I'M NOT GOING OVER THIS AGAIN, HANK," my father was saying. "This conversation was finished yesterday."

"But *this* conversation is not *that* conversation," I tried to explain. "Well, it is kind of like that conversation, but it's not exactly that conversation. This conversation has a whole new twist."

We were in our living room and my dad was doing a crossword puzzle in his La-Z-Boy chair in the medium-recline position. That's his favorite position except when he's watching *Jeopardy!*, when he goes into full recline. He says leaning back helps the blood get to his head so his brain thinks of the answers faster. I tried it once when I had to study for a geography test and had to learn all the capitals of the African continent. All that blood rushing to my head just made me dizzy.

"You wait right here, Dad. Don't change

locations. I'll be right back."

I raced into the kitchen where my mom was paying the Crunchy Pickle bills at the kitchen table. I took her by the hand and pulled her out of the chair.

"Family meeting," I said to her as I led her into the living room. "This might be one of the most important family meetings we'll ever have."

I left her in the living room, and then raced down the hall to Emily's bedroom. She was feeding Katherine lettuce burgers, which is two pieces of lettuce with a piece of balled-up lettuce in the middle.

"What now?" she said, without looking up.

"I need you desperately," I said.

"So does Katherine. We're in the middle of snack time."

"Emily, I promise that once Katherine finds out what this is all about, she'll be so happy you came with me."

"If I come with you, Katherine comes, too."

"Fine. Just tell her to keep the hissing down and her tongue to herself."

Emily picked Katherine up and the gruesome twosome followed me into the living room. We gathered around my dad's La-Z-Boy.

"I'm sure you're all wondering why I called this emergency family meeting," I began.

"Not really," said Emily. "In fact, not at all."

"I made a deal with Dad that I'd get a B-plus on my math test or I couldn't be in the play. But we all know that even the father of our country, George Washington, sometimes had to go back to his dad and reconsider a decision, like that whole chopping down the cherry tree thing."

"That's a very good use of history, honey," my mom said. She always looks at the positive side of things.

"Well, if George's dad had grounded him, he wouldn't have learned how to ride a horse, which means he wouldn't have become a general, because generals had to ride on their white horses in front of the troops. And that means he wouldn't have been president, and then we wouldn't have the Constitution, which gives us freedom of speech, which we're using right here today in Apartment 10A."

Katherine hissed. No, she couldn't be having a hissy fit when I was making the most important argument of my life. That was unacceptable.

"Excuse us," Emily said with a giggle.

"Come on, Emily. This is important to me. Focus."

"Look who's talking."

"So I've been thinking about this," I went on, "and I'd like to ask that we reconsider Dad's decision. I know the material on that test. I spent hours with Heather going over and over it. I just messed up because that's how I do things."

"Stanley, he has a point," my mom said. "Dr. Berger has told us that Hank gets nervous in testing situations."

You go, Mom!

"Randi, you're making excuses again," my dad answered.

"Let me finish, Dad. Here's my idea. To show you that I really do know my long division, I suggest I take a test right now. You can make up the problem. If I get it right, it counts as a B-plus. If I get it wrong, I'll never bring this up again."

"I think Hank is making a very fair proposal," my mom said. "What do you say, Stanley?"

"I have to agree with Mom," I chimed in, answering for my dad.

"Your mother is willing to make too many

allowances for you, Hank. I can't do that any-more. Sometimes the toughest lessons are what make you the strongest."

"Stanley," my mom said. "I don't want to disagree with you in front of the kids, but if Hank can prove to us that he really knows his math, then it seems fair to me that we give him that chance."

My dad was quiet.

"I agree with Mom," Emily said. "I honestly think that Hank's got a good idea, for the first time in six and a half years. The last one was when he put apple juice in the sand castle moat that we built at Jones Beach."

"I remember that," my mom said. "It attract-ed all those lovely sand crabs."

"Were they hermit crabs or fiddler crabs?" my sister the science nerd asked.

"No crab talk, Emily," I barked. "I'm really trying to focus here. How about if we take a vote?"

"Well, I vote yes," my mom said.

"I can't believe it, but I vote yes, too," Emily said. Katherine opened her mouth and shot her tongue out in the direction of my cheek.

"I think Katherine just gave me a lizard

kiss," I said, "which we all agree has to count as a yes vote. So there you have it, Dad. Majority rules."

My dad pushed the lever of his chair, and he shot upright into a sitting position.

"Unfortunately, Hank, this family is not a democracy."

Suddenly, my father got up and walked over to the dining room table. He didn't say a word, just pulled his mechanical pencil from his shirt pocket, grabbed a yellow pad of paper, and started to write. I didn't move a muscle.

When he came back, he placed the yellow pad and pencil down on the coffee table. There it was. One nifty long division problem smiling up at me. My whole future rested on four hundred and ninety-seven divided by seven.

"You get the right answer, you can be in the play," my dad said. "Begin."

I looked at the problem and the numbers started to dance around on the page like they always do. But I picked up the pad with both hands and held it tight, forcing my eyes to focus on the numbers on the page.

Come on, eyes! You're not just there to be brown and cute. Now read!

I reviewed the steps Heather had taught me. First step. Seven goes into forty-nine how many times? Is it five? Or six? Or seven?

I'll take six. It's in the middle.

I wrote down a six on the paper. I looked up at everyone staring at me. I thought maybe one of them would nod their head if I was on the right track. There was no nodding going on.

Cheerio could feel the tension, I guess, because he started to chase his tail. I kept watching him spin around and around. My mom could see that I was losing focus, so she picked Cheerio up and started to scratch him behind the ears.

I wish someone would scratch me behind the ears. I could use a little calming down.

I took a deep breath, remembering that oxygen is power, and looked at the problem again.

Come on, brain. Join the team. You can kick in anytime you want. We're all waiting.

Wait a minute! It's not six, it's seven. Seven goes into forty-nine seven times! I erased the six without tearing the paper, and changed it to a seven. I looked up at my mom. Now I thought I saw a little nodding going on.

Come on, brain, don't fail me now.

My pencil flew across the paper, bringing

down numbers in nice neat columns, subtracting, dividing again, multiplying again. After a few minutes, I had an answer. Seventy-one.

I handed the yellow pad to my father. My stomach did backflips while he looked over my work. It seemed to take forever.

And in case you're like me and not too swift in the math department, let me just announce to you now that four hundred and ninety-seven divided by seven equals . . .

. . . *ta-da* . . .

. . . seventy-one!!!

CHAPTER 22

WHEN WE GOT TO SCHOOL the next morning, Frankie, Ashley, and I went directly to the multi-purpose room. McKelty had already been named the king, and I wasn't sure whether Devore would let me back into the play.

When we walked in, Nick McKelty was standing on the stage, wearing my costume. Devore was supervising Mrs. Crock, who was kneeling in front of McKelty, putting pins in the golden pantaloons. Oh no, it looked like they had already added more fabric to make the pants stretch around McKelty's tree-trunklike waist. My heart started to sink. I was too late.

I raced over to Devore.

"My father said yes," I blurted out.

Devore looked at Mrs. Crock, who was kneeling down with a mouthful of pins, working on letting out the pantaloons. She had turned McKelty around, so his big bubble butt was staring us right in the face. Wow, it took a lot to cover up that big, round thing. I didn't know there was that much gold fabric in all of New York.

"I thought your father forbid you," Devore said to me.

"It's a long story," I said. "But he finally said yes."

Devore was quiet, not jumping up and down with joy like I had hoped he would.

"But the costume . . ." Devore said, his voice trailing off. "And yesterday, we changed some of the staging."

Mrs. Crock turned McKelty another quarter turn, so he was now facing us. Poor lady had run out of pins.

"Hey, Zipperbutt, check me out," McKelty said. "Now you can finally see what a king is supposed to look like. I was born to wear gold."

Devore looked at him.

"Lots of important producers have already called, asking me to leave school and star in their Broadway plays," Nick went on, giving Devore a blast of the McKelty factor at work. "But I'm going to leave them all dangling for a while. Give Hollywood a chance to call—then weigh my offers."

"That does it," Devore said, like he had just

awakened from a horrible dream. "Mr. McKelty, thank you so much for filling in during Hank's absence, but as in the real theater, the understudy must step aside when the original star is able to return."

"Huh?" McKelty said.

"You're fired, dude," Frankie said.

"You can't fire me," McKelty said.

"Might I remind you that I am the director," Devore said. "I must do what's right for the play."

"So hand over the costume, McKelty," Ashley said. "It's going on Hank's royal body now."

"About that," Mrs. Crock said to Devore. "The costume has already been altered significantly to make it fit Nick."

"Don't worry about that, Mrs. Crock," I said. "I'll use a belt to hold up the pants."

"But the King of Siam wouldn't have worn a belt," Devore said.

"How about this?" Ashley said, pointing to a golden cord with two tassels that was draped over the back of the throne. And without waiting for an answer, she pulled the cord off the throne and brought it to Devore. "We can use it to hold up the pants."

"Now that, my dear, is thinking like a true theater person," Devore said.

"So what happens to me?" McKelty said. "I'm just supposed to fade into the background like this never happened?"

"There's a plan." Frankie laughed.

Devore ignored his remark and rubbed his goatee thoughtfully before he spoke. "As a gesture of our appreciation," he began, "for your . . . um . . ."

"Talent?" Nick filled in.

"Let's just say, for your unique understudy skills," Devore said, "it would be a pleasure to ask you to join Luke Whitman and play Elephant Boy Number Two."

"Is it a speaking part?" McKelty asked.

"No, but your presence on the stage will speak volumes," Devore said.

"He'll take it," Frankie answered for McKelty.

"But aren't I still the understudy?" McKelty asked.

"Indeed you are," Devore told him.

"Because something awful could still happen to Zipperbutt, right?" McKelty said. "I mean, you never know what could happen. The theater is a strange place."

Don't ask me why, but I didn't like the sound of that.

CHAPTER 23

ON THE NIGHT OF THE MUSICAL, the multi-purpose room was full of parents and grand-parents, little brothers, older sisters, and about as many video cameras as there were people. Everyone in the audience was scrambling for seats and calling out to friends. The entire room was buzzing with electricity. All of the cast members could feel it, most of all me, because I was the one peeking out from behind the red velvet curtain that Devore had insisted we hang across the stage.

It was just before showtime. As I stood behind the curtain, my right eye, or maybe it was my left, scanned the room like a periscope on a submarine. I was searching for the Zipzer family. I found Papa Pete first, because he was wearing his bright red running suit, which makes him stand out in a crowd. My mom and Emily were there, sitting next to Robert Upchurch and his mom. Thank goodness, Emily and Robert had left Katherine at home. She doesn't do well in crowds. And by the way, neither does my dad. He was looking seriously uncomfortable, pulling at his tie. I couldn't hear him clearing his throat nervously, but I knew he was.

"It's very unprofessional to peek through the curtain before showtime," Devore said to me. "It's just not done. But while you're at it, do we have a full house?"

"Standing room only," I reported to him.

"I sense we have a hit on our hands, my boy," Devore said. "Now take your place on the throne."

"I'm on my way," I said. "But first, Devore, can you answer just one question for me?"

"Of course."

"What's my first line? I've completely forgotten it."

Devore didn't panic. He didn't really need to, because I was panicked enough for both of us.

"This is a normal and natural occurrence," Devore said, "that happens to many of us theater professionals."

"And what do we theater professionals do when our brains dry up like a prune?" I asked.

"We do not worry," Devore said. "You knew

your lines during dress rehearsal, and you'll know them when the curtain goes up. Your muse will come."

I had no idea what a muse was, but I couldn't wait for it to get there, because it was showtime, which is no time for a muse to be late.

As I took my place on the throne, Heather came running out from stage left. That's a theater term that means I have no idea which side she was coming from. The good thing was that she was there onstage. I hoped she saw my muse on the way out.

Heather looked really good. She had undone her braids so her hair was falling on her shoulders. She was wearing a long blue dress that went all the way down to the floor. It had a hoop around the bottom that made it stick out in a big circle around her.

Note to self. Do not step on that hoop when we dance. That is a trip waiting to happen.

Heather took her place by the door where she was supposed to make her entrance. Wait a minute. What was wrong with her? She wasn't walking like a human. She looked like a marble statue moving stiffly across the stage.

"Are you okay?" I whispered to her.

She opened her mouth to answer me, but all that came out was a squeak.

Great. My brain is dried up like a prune, and her voice box has gone on vacation to Hawaii. We're going to be quite a pair.

"Don't worry, Heather," I said. "Your muse will fix everything. He must be stuck in traffic . . . with mine."

When she looked at me, all I could see was panic in her eyes.

"Okay, Heather, we can do this," I said, absolutely not believing a word of my own hot air. "Remember to breathe in and out. Keep saying 'I am relaxed.'"

She started to breathe, but not deep breaths. They were quick little shallow ones, coming so fast that I think she started to get dizzy. I noticed her swaying on her feet for no reason.

"Wow, I didn't know what a great breather you were," I said to her. "I'm pretty positive that's enough breathing for now."

Just at that moment, a piano chord blared loud and strong from beyond the curtain. It was Mr. Rock, starting the musical introduction to let the audience know that the play was about to begin.

Thank you, Mr. Rock! We have to move fast before Heather passes out completely.

"Places, everyone," Frankie said, bringing all the kindergarten kids out onto the stage. They were playing the king's nineteen children, and they looked so cute in their little pantaloons. I noticed that my favorite kindergarten pal, Mason, was wearing his Power Ranger flip-flops, which probably didn't exist hundreds of years ago in Siam, but he looked pretty cool in them, anyway. Frankie talked into his headset, making sure Ryan Shimozato and the other king's guards had their swords ready when the curtain went up. As he ran by me, he put his hand up for a high five and whispered, "Knock 'em out, dude." I glanced at Heather. She already looked knocked out.

I climbed onto my throne and adjusted the gold cord I was using to hold up my pantaloons. There had been no time to sew me new pants, so they were still McKelty-size. Fortunately, the belt Ashley had created from the cord was working fine. I pulled it tighter around my waist, just to make sure everything stayed where it was supposed to stay.

"Hard pants to fill, huh, Zipperclown?" McKelty whispered as he settled in next to Luke

Whitman on the stage. "I look better in that costume, anyway."

"Yeah, especially if it's covering your face," Ashley whispered from her place at the curtain. Now that she was done with the costume design, her job was to raise and lower the curtain.

"Break a leg, moron," McKelty said to me. "In fact, break three."

"Hey, good luck to you, too, McKelty," I said, wondering why he was calling me a moron when he was the one who thought people had three legs.

There was no time for more conversation, because just then, Devore stepped through the slit in the curtain and took his place in front of the audience. The room was totally quiet now. I could hear myself breathing.

"Ladies and gentlemen," Devore said, in a voice so big that it flew up to the ceiling and bounced off all the walls before it landed in your ears. "I invite you to come with us now to the ancient land of Siam, where we find that the king has hired Anna, an English tutor, to instruct his children in the ways of the western world."

Devore wiggled two fingers in back of him, which was Ashley's cue to start raising the curtain. Devore exited stage right. Or maybe it was stage left. Don't ask me. The point is, he exited and came to stand in the wings in case we needed him.

As the curtain went up, I looked out at the audience. Wow, that was a lot of people. You could hear all the parents' video cameras humming at once. I just sat there on my throne, frozen solid like a pineapple Popsicle on a stick.

Okay, Hankster. You have the first line. Now go. Speak. Take it away.

I opened my mouth and nothing came out. Heather was standing with her suitcase, ready for me to speak to her.

Like I was saying, Hankster. Anytime you want to say your first line, be my guest.

Again, nothing.

I glanced over at Frankie, who was standing in the wings. Heather was waiting. Luke Whitman and Nick McKelty stood in their elephant boy costumes, holding the door open for her. Ryan Shimozato and the guards had their swords drawn. The kindergarten kids wiggled and scratched their noses. One of them giggled and waved to her mom in the front row.

"Welcome to my palace," Frankie mouthed.

*That's sounding familiar. I wonder why? Oh,
right. It's my first line.*

I opened my mouth and out came the
words.

"Welcome to my palace, Anna," I finally
said.

*Yes! I was off and running. This wasn't so
hard.*

"My dear Anna, you must have had a long
and tiring journey."

*I was on a roll, acting up a complete storm.
It was fun.*

"I am honored to be in the presence of your
highness," Heather answered. There they were,
those words, coming out of her mouth just
like they were in the script, just like we had
rehearsed!

Hey, look at us. Now we're both acting.

"The elephant boy will take your suitcase," I
said, really starting to enjoy the moment. "Oh,
elephant boy, please show Miss Anna to her
quarters, where she can freshen up before she
meets the children."

Heather turned to Nick McKelty and handed
him her suitcase. He was supposed to take the
suitcase and lead her offstage. But could that big

hambone ever do only what he was supposed to do?

"Let me give your suitcase to my assistant," McKelty bellowed, which was definitely not a line in the script.

With that, McKelty grabbed the suitcase from Heather and tossed it to Luke Whitman, who wasn't expecting it. It hit Luke in the stomach and knocked him over like a bowling pin.

The audience laughed, but Devore didn't. I saw him standing in the wings. And if you ever wondered what a human being looks like just before his face explodes, leaving only his ears attached, that was Devore. He wagged his finger at McKelty, and although it was meant as a warning, I'm sure from the look on McKelty's face he took it as Devore complimenting him on his acting.

I wasn't sure what to do, but since Devore had always told us that the play must go on, on I went. I leaped off my throne and walked to the center of the stage. I bowed good-bye to Anna, hoping that Heather would be able to improvise a good-bye and then just leave with Luke Whitman. As you know, she's not a great improviser.

I turned to face her and bent over to begin my bow. First I swept both my arms up into the air, and then I brought them down so that my hands rested on my hips. I had seen the actor in the movie do that, and it had looked pretty darn great. As I took my bow, I was willing to bet that a lot of the audience actually thought I came from Siam.

The next thing I knew, as I was completing my bow, McKelty shot out to the middle of the stage, next to me.

"Here, my king," he bellowed. "Let me help you with that."

Help me? With what?

Before I knew what was happening, he grabbed the end of the gold cord that was holding up my pants and tugged it with all his might. I started to spin like a top. For the first time in my life, I knew how Cheerio felt when he chased his tail. When I stopped spinning, I was clear across the stage. I noticed a cool breeze floating across my legs. I reached down and felt around for the gold cord. It wasn't there.

I looked down and realized that my golden pantaloons had fallen down and were lying in a heap at my feet. The only thing between me and the audience were my polka-dotted Mets boxer briefs.

I was in shock. Devore was in shock. Mr. Rock stopped playing. He was in shock. The only person whose face I could pick out in the audience was Ms. Adolf. And believe me, she was totally in shock. She put her program on her head like a hat, covering her eyes with the pages.

I looked over at Frankie, who was standing in the wings. For maybe the first time ever in his life, he had no idea what to do. I looked to Ashley, who was standing by the curtain, hoping that she would have the sense to lower it and end this horrible embarrassment. But she must have been in shock, too, because she just stood there and started twirling her ponytail nervously. All the kindergarten kids cracked up, even my pal Mason.

There I was, standing with my golden pantaloons around my ankles. Should I step out of them and run away? Or should I bend over to pull them up? Bending over didn't seem like a good choice. So I just stood there. Suddenly, somebody's little brother in the front row screamed as loud as he could, "Look, Mommy.

He's got the same underpants I do."

The audience roared with laughter. Out of the corner of my eye, I could see that Devore had dropped to his knees. He was holding his cape over his eyes. I think he was crying. No, sobbing. Nick McKelty was laughing his head off. The golden cord that had once held up my pants was in his chubby, grubby hand.

As for me, all I could do was wave.

Why I didn't just hop off the stage and run all the way to California without stopping will always be one of the great mysteries of my life. All I can tell you is that no thoughts occurred to me. Not one little tiny one.

I promise you that in a million trillion years, you will never guess what happened next.

Stiff Heather Payne, the same girl who could not say a line that wasn't written and memorized, the non-improviser of all non-improvisers, stepped into the spotlight and took total command of the situation.

It was as if Anna had suddenly come alive in her. Her muse had arrived! Heather twirled herself in her blue hoop skirt over to Luke Whitman and grabbed the suitcase from his hands. Then she twirled over to me. With a huge flourish, she threw open the suitcase lid and reached inside, producing a blue shawl that matched her dress.

She wrapped the shawl around my waist like a magic trick, then wound it around me so it looked like one of those long skirts that an ancient king of Siam might actually wear.

"Your highness, I didn't want you to catch a cold," she said as she was twirling and wrapping, wrapping and twirling. "So I brought you this garment from my land—Eng . . . land."

Wow. Was this Heather Payne? It looked like her. It was as tall as her. But it sure didn't sound like her.

"And you, elephant boy," she said, turning to Nick McKelty. "Return to the stables and tend to the animals. One of the elephants has a runny trunk and needs to have it wiped immediately."

Even a big mouth like McKelty's couldn't come up with an answer for that! Heather Payne was improvising her brains out. There was no doubt about it. All McKelty could do was slink off the stage.

With McKelty gone and my tush safely wrapped up in a shawl, I was on the way back from Embarrassmentville. The audience had even stopped laughing. That was the good news.

even stopped laughing. That was the good news. The bad news was I had no idea what to do next. Everyone was waiting.

I opened my mouth and just prayed something good would come out. Devore had said that my muse would take over. This couldn't have been a better time for it to show up.

"Anna, I feel so kingly wearing this elegant gift from you," I said with a flourish. "In fact, I feel like dancing, if you know what I mean."

"Yes, your highness, I know exactly what you mean," she said with a big smile.

I turned to Mr. Rock and said, "Palace musicians, I command you to play."

Mr. Rock picked up my cue and launched into the introduction to the dance number that Heather and I had rehearsed for two weeks.

"Anna," I said, with a low bow. "Shall we dance?"

"My pleasure, your highness."

I put one hand around her waist, and just to make sure that my Mets boxer briefs were not going to make a repeat appearance, kept my other hand tightly clutched to the shawl wrapped around me.

Heather and I took off, twirling around the

stage. Let me tell you, our rehearsals really paid off. We didn't miss a step. We were in perfect harmony. And before we knew it, the audience was clapping in time to the music and cheering as we danced around the stage.

On our final turn, I caught Ashley's eye and gave her the nod. She knew what I meant because she lowered the curtain as we spun around the stage for our final turn. Through the curtain, we could hear the audience cheering and stomping their feet.

I looked over at Devore. He had stopped crying. In fact, he was laughing.

So was Heather.

And so was I!

CHAPTER 24

TEN FANTABULOUS COMPLIMENTS I GOT FOR PLAYING THE KING

1. Heather Payne said I taught her how to improvise and I was the best peer tutor a person could ever have.
2. With a compliment like that, who needs the other nine?

About the Authors

HENRY WINKLER is an actor, producer, and director, and he speaks publicly all over the world. Holy mackerel! No wonder he needs a nap. He lives in Los Angeles with his wife, Stacey. They have three children named Jed, Zoe, and Max, and two dogs named Monty and Charlotte. If you gave him one word to describe how he feels about this book, he would say "proud."

If you gave him two words, he would say "I am so happy that I got a chance to write this book with Lin and I really hope you enjoy it." That's twenty-two words, but hey, he's got learning challenges.

LIN OLIVER is a writer and producer of movies, books, and television series for children and families. She has created over one hundred episodes of television, four movies, and seven books. She lives in Los Angeles with her husband, Alan. They have three sons named Theo, Ollie, and Cole, and a very adorable but badly behaved puppy named Dexter.

If you gave her two words to describe this book, she would say "funny and compassionate." If you asked her what compassionate meant, she would say "full of kindness." She would not make you look it up in the dictionary.